Eighteen Bowties and Counting

Christian Cowboy Romance

Three Rivers Ranch Romance
Book 18

Liz Isaacson

ISBN-13: 978-1-63876-361-1

Reader Note

Hello Fabulous Christian Cowboy Readers!

I'm thrilled you're back in Three Rivers with me!

This is a mini-age gap cowboy romance with a "one cabin," grumpy sunshine trope - where she's the grump! I think you're going to LOVE Beau and Charlotte.

In it, you'll get sweet and swoony kisses and nothing more. An amazing pet name for Charlotte from Beau.

And the super-sizzling trope of "one cabin!" That's right. Charlotte and Beau are forced to live together in the foreman's cabin at Three Rivers Ranch!

Charlotte has a minor heart condition, which has put a major chip on her shoulder. She's tired of being babied and protected, and she's a little salty, with high walls, sometimes. All of my books address real life situations without fear or shame, because I believe we all make mistakes, our Savior suffered for all of us, and we can all repent, be healed, and come back to God.

So are you ready for true-to-life romance, family saga, and the small town goodness you might've come to expect from Three Rivers?! I hope so! If you're new, you're in for a treat!

xoxo

~Liz

The Small Town of Three Rivers

Welcome to Three Rivers! There have been three complete series here already - Three Rivers Ranch, Seven Sons Ranch (Walker Brothers), and Shiloh Ridge Ranch (Glover Family).

That's 37 books. Loads of characters. I'm going to list them here, but you don't need to know them all comprehensively for this book. I just know some of you like seeing these amazing small towns and who lives here!

Three Rivers Ranch:

Frank and Heidi Ackerman - patriarch and matriarch. Frank died 15 years ago; Heidi is remarried to Malcolm Rust.

Squire and Kelly Ackerman

Son: Finn - 21
Daughter: Libby - 15
Son: Michael - 13
Son: Samuel - 9

Pete and Chelsea Marshall (Chelsea is Squire's sister, and they own Courage Reins, which is housed at Three Rivers Ranch)

4 sons:
Paul - 15
Henry - 14
John - 11
Rich - 8

Reese and Carly Sanders: They're the admins for Courage Reins, Pete and Chelsea's equine therapy unit at Three Rivers Ranch. They have no children.

Garth and Juliette Ahlstrom (former foreman; vet technician)

Son: Jake - 13
Son: Carson - 11

Cal and Trina Hodgkins (he's the full-time vet at Three Rivers Ranch)

Daughter: Sabrina - 24
Daughter: Abby - 14
Daughter: Olive - 11

Ethan and Brynn Greene (they own Bowman's Breeds, which is housed at Three Rivers Ranch)
Daughter: Carolina - 13
Son: Tyson - 11
Son: Bryan - 9

Beau Peterson (foreman at Three Rivers Ranch), single

Bennett and Ellie Peterson (he's a cowboy, she works on the finances on the ranch with Kelly)

Tad and Sandy Jorgensen (he's a cowboy, she owns the pancake house in town)
Son: Nathaniel (Nate) - 11
Daughter: Helen - 8

Kenny and Taryn Stockton (he's a cowboy, she works for a local online newspaper in town)
Daughter: Joelle (Jo) - 10

. . .

Jon and Grace Carver (he's a cowboy, she helps Heidi run the bakery in town)

Andy and Lawrence Collins (he's a cowboy, she owns a clothing boutique in town)

Summer and Tanner Wolfe (he's a cowboy, she's a nurse at the hospital in town)

Gavin and Navy Redd - they own their own single-family ranch on the northeast side of Three Rivers

Boone and Nicole Carver (Squire's cousin) - they own and operate the full time veterinary clinic in town

Camila and Dylan Walker (he's a cowboy and an electrician, she owns a plumbing shop in town)

Seven Sons Ranch:

Momma & Daddy: Penny and Gideon Walker

1. RHETT & EVELYN WALKER
Son: Conrad - 12
Triplets: Austin, Elaine, and Easton - 8

2. JEREMIAH & WHITNEY WALKER
Son: Jonah Jeremiah (JJ) - 10
Daughter: Clara Jean - 8
Son: Jason - 6
Daughter: Emily - 4
Daughter: Hattie - 1

3. LIAM & CALLIE WALKER
Daughter: Denise - 16
Daughter: Ginger - 12

4. TRIPP & IVORY WALKER
Son: Oliver - 24 (and married to Aurora Glover)
Son: Isaac - 12

5. WYATT & MARCY WALKER
Son: Warren - 9
Son: Cole - 7
Son: Harrison - 6
Daughter: Rachel - 3

. . .

6. Skyler & Mallery Walker
    Daughter: Camila - 9
    Son: Sawyer - 7
    Son: Gideon - 4

7. Micah & Simone Walker
    Son: Travis (Trap) - 8
    Daughter: Daisy - 6
    Son: Jensen - 2
    Daughter: Laurel - newborn

Shiloh Ridge Ranch:
   Lois & Stone (deceased) Glover, 7 children, in age-order: (Lois is now married to Donald Parker)
   1. Bear — Sammy, wife

   - Lincoln (18), adopted son
   - Stetson (Smiles, 7), son
   - Russell (Rock, 6), son
   - Heather (4), daughter
   - Sunnie (3), daughter

   2. Cactus — Allison, ex-wife / Bryce, son (deceased) // — Willa, wife

- Mitch (17), adopted son
- Cameron (12), adopted son
- Kyle (10), adopted son
- Charlie (Chaz, 8), son
- Lynn (7), adopted daughter
- Melissa (4), daughter

3. Judge — June, wife

- Lucy Mae (22), step-daughter
- Birch (5), son
- Willow (2), daughter

4. Preacher — Charlie, wife

- Betty (5), daughter
- Hank (2), son

5. Arizona — Duke Rhinehart, husband, living at the Rhinehart Ranch, just south of Shiloh Ridge

- Shiloh (6), daughter
- April (3), daughter
- Dwayne (1), son

6. Mister — Libby, wife

- Belle (3), son
- Marley (1), daughter

7. Bishop — Montana, wife

- Aurora (24), step-daughter and married to Oliver Osburn
- Robbie (10), son
- Georgia (3), daughter

Dawna & Bull (deceased) Glover, 5 children, in age-order:

1. Ranger — Oakley, wife

- Wilder (7), son
- Fawn (6), daughter

2. Ward — Dot, wife

- Glory Rose (7), daughter
- Silver (4), son
- Flint (2), son

3. Ace — Holly Ann, wife

- Gunnison (6), son
- Pearl Jo (4), daughter
- Ashton (1), son

4. Etta — August Winters, husband

- Hailey (14), adopted daughter
- Joey (4), son
- Nash and Nellie (twins - 2), son and daughter

5. Ida — Brady Burton, husband

- Johnny and Judy (twins - 7), son and daughter
- Riggs (2), son

. . .

Bull and Stone Glover were brothers, so their children are cousins. Ranger and Bear, for example, are cousins, and each the oldest sibling in their families.

Chapter One

Beau Peterson poured himself a cup of coffee, the feeling down deep inside him starting to bubble to the surface. He hadn't decided if it was a good feeling or a bad one, and he glanced over to the clock ticking away in his kitchen.

His parents had owned it, but it had originally belonged to his grandfather on his dad's side. So the grandfather clock seemed fitting. It told time precisely, and if Beau knew his best friend, Bennett would be arriving any minute.

He stirred sugar into his coffee and lifted the hot liquid to his lips, his gaze skating by the championship photos of his younger sister and the horses she used to show. The coffee stung bitterly against his tongue, and he went back to get more sweetener. The first chime on the clock had just sounded when Bennett knocked on the front door and opened it at the same time.

"Ah, coffee," he said, his grin permanently in place these

days. And why shouldn't it be? The man was getting married this weekend.

Ruby lifted her head from where she lay on the couch, her breakfast long gone. Pepper, Beau's black lab, jumped down from his pre-work nap to greet Bennett.

Beau glanced past the man he'd lived with and worked with for just about twenty years now. Of course he was happy for Bennett and his soon-to-be-bride. He absolutely was. He'd show up on the day and play the part—and heaven knew Beau had been a best man or a groomsman enough to do his duties in his sleep.

The seventeen bowties hanging from the long two-by-four in the hallway spoke of that. Bennett had made the display for him one day last year; he'd made one for himself too. Before he'd met Ellie. Before they'd started dating. Before things got serious.

Beau had no idea where his best friend's bowties had gone. His still hung in the hallway of the foreman's cabin, where he'd moved six months ago when he'd become the foreman of Three Rivers Ranch.

Bennett threw a box on the counter. "Look what I got for you." He bent down to scratch Pepper's ears, cooing at the dog like he was a baby instead of a seven-year-old black lab with gray starting to grow around his mouth.

Beau took another taste of his coffee instead of looking at anything. Neither of them wore their cowboy hats inside, so Beau's raised eyebrows landed squarely on Bennett as he poured himself a cup of coffee as if they still lived together.

Beau could admit that it had been hard living alone. He'd

never really done it, and his momma had told him for the entirety of his life that he wasn't meant to be alone. He did have the two dogs, and he had a small herd of donkeys who brayed and brayed whenever he found time to go visit them. If three could be considered a herd. To Beau, it was, and he was the only one calling them that anyway.

Too bad he'd never been able to find anyone to get serious with, the way Bennett had. And Squire. Pete. Brett. Tom. Garth. Reese. Ethan.

The list went on and on. Times seventeen.

Seventeen weddings he'd attended. Seventeen wedding parties. Seventeen bow ties.

Dear Lord, he thought. *Will it ever be my turn?*

God did not answer, and Beau hadn't really been trying to find anyone anyway. Not since his new job appointment, that was. Running a ranch the size of Three Rivers was the job of at least six men, and Beau was still learning the ropes despite having lived and worked on this ranch for a couple decades now.

"Are you going to look?" Bennett asked, drawing Beau back to the kitchen. Back to the present. Back to his current loneliness.

He reached over and picked up the box, knowing exactly what it was. Only one thing came in a frilly blue box with silver engraving on the top.

Sure enough, a purple bowtie sat inside, and Beau forced a smile to his face. "For the wedding," he said needlessly.

Bennett must've heard something in Beau's voice, because he swept the bowtie away. Before he could even blink, Bennett had his fingers curled around the back of his neck. "I'm sorry," he whispered.

"It's fine," Beau said back. No questions needed. He knew exactly what Bennett was apologizing for, and they both knew it wasn't fine. Sure, they'd been flirtatious and maybe even considered playboys back in the day.

Both of them had gone out with any number of women. Beau couldn't even pinpoint exactly when he'd decided he'd had enough of the fun-loving dating life. When he'd wanted to find a single woman he could fall deeply in love with and build a life with. It felt like it had been eight or nine years now, but time had warped in a lot of ways.

For example, Beau couldn't believe that shortly following Ben's wedding, he'd turn forty.

Him.

Forty.

Still single.

Texting his momma that he was still alive, still liked West Texas more than New Mexico, still missed his daddy like crazy, and no, still hadn't found anyone to call his.

Bennett pulled his hand back and cleared his throat. "Where we at today?"

"Well, I have some paperwork to go over in the admin trailer," Beau said, the words accompanied with a big sigh. "Then I'm gonna help with the loft tear-out in the hay barn, and then I have interviews this afternoon for the new Stable Master."

Ben nodded and nodded. "Where'd you put me?"

"Not anywhere you'd get sunburnt or hurt, I know that." Beau grinned at his best friend, most of the melancholy melting clean away. "Ellie would never forgive me if I let you show up to your wedding in a cast or looking like Rudolph."

Ben laughed, and it felt good for Beau to join his voice in with his friend's. He didn't ask if Beau had found a date to the wedding. If he had, he'd have texted Ben to say so. He didn't ask if he'd be there to calm him down only minutes before the ceremony began. Of course he would be.

He didn't ask if Beau would be okay once Ben had moved off the ranch to Ellie's house in town. He wouldn't be—neither of them would be. So many changes had entered their lives in the past year, and Beau had to remind himself daily that change was good. Change encouraged growth. Change could get a cowboy moving in the direction he was meant to be moving.

Simultaneously, Beau felt utterly suspended in time, unable to move forward or backward, left or right, up or down. Nothing.

"Let's get goin'," he said, mostly because he'd seen the concern enter Ben's eyes just now. He didn't want to answer any more questions, and he didn't need another apology. Ben shouldn't even have to apologize for meeting a great woman, falling in love with her, and getting married.

This weekend.

You can make it through one more wedding, he told himself. *One more weekend. No big deal.*

Maybe if he recited it enough, it would somehow be true.

"Come on, dogs," he said to Ruby and Pepper. "Time to get to work." His faithful pups trotted out with him, Bennett hot on their heels, and as Beau took a taste of the morning air, he decided his life wasn't all bad just because he didn't have a girlfriend.

Hours later, with hay seemingly clinging to every part of his body, Beau made his way back to the cabin on the end of the row. The biggest, nicest one, where the foreman lived. He had three bedrooms, a loft, and two baths in addition to a bigger living room, dining room, and kitchen. Oh, and a full deck off the back door. A real back lawn. A real front one too, which none of the other cowboys had.

The foreman's cabin sat the furthest from the homestead and the closest to the administration building. It was shielded from the worst of the animal smells on the ranch, the loudest of the squabbling chickens, and all of the traffic that came to the ranch for riding lessons, equine therapy appointments, rodeo horses, and any other business on the ranch.

Beau had finished his paperwork quickly that morning, which meant he'd been working in the hay barn, tearing out the rotted and soft wood in the loft, for long enough to be starving, dirty, sweaty, and covered in what felt like hay splinters up and down his arms.

"Despite wearing a long-sleeved shirt," he muttered. He headed toward his cabin, ready for a shower and something to eat. He checked his phone as his cowboy boots crunched over the immaculate gravel running in front of the row of cowboy cabins, and which separated the housing of men and women from the housing of horses, chickens, and even a few pigs.

Ducks, dogs, cats, and even calves sometimes. Three Rivers Ranch had it all.

Beau made the turn to go down the short sidewalk to his front steps, and he'd gained them all when he realized his front door stood open a few inches. He immediately slowed, though having someone come to the foreman's cabin certainly wasn't all that abnormal.

He'd had a nasty head cold a few months ago, and he'd conducted all his business from home, through texts, or not at all.

But today, he wasn't expecting anyone until after lunch. He wanted to put a pizza in the oven, take a fast shower to scrub the hay shards from his skin, and prep for the interviews.

A visitor? Not on the agenda, and Beau's irritation grew as he stepped lightly toward his door.

He used a couple of fingers to nudge the door open further, now annoyed that his air conditioning—which he had to pay for, thank you very much—had been leaking out and cooling the brutal Texas July.

His gaze immediately got drawn to the blonde woman standing in front of his grandfather clock. Pepper surely saw her too, as he darted inside to go greet their visitor. The black lab loved people as much as he loved tennis balls, sticks, and the blue Frisbee Beau threw for him every night. Well, every night the wind wasn't howling behind the cabin. So most nights.

The woman didn't turn from the clock—or perhaps the pictures on the credenza beside it—to greet Pepper, much to the canine's displeasure. Beau wasn't entirely sure what she was looking at. He knew she shouldn't be in his house, but he paused in the doorway to watch her for some reason.

She sure seemed familiar to him, but he couldn't quite be sure as she hadn't faced him fully yet. Her long, blonde hair hung a few inches past her shoulders, and she wore her cowgirl hat inside. Blue jeans. A blue shirt that looked like she might have bought it from the men's section at The Boot Barn. A pair of sturdy work boots.

Ruby, his collie, trotted over to the woman too, and as she stood a little taller than Pepper, and she definitely had more fluff, she brushed up against the woman's hand. She sucked in a breath, looked down at the dog, and seemed to sway on her feet.

Or maybe the earth had moved.

Because Beau suddenly recognized her. With that slight tilt of her head toward him, as the woman looked down at the collie, he knew her.

Charlotte Wisenhouer.

He hadn't seen her in forever—clearly. She'd grown all the way up, and he reminded himself he wasn't a twenty-year-old anymore, flirting with anyone wearing a lipglossed smile and earrings.

And Charlotte had been off-limits for as long as he could remember anyway. Her older brother Mason was Beau's age, and he'd warned Beau away from Charlotte years ago.

What in the world was she doing here now? Standing in his cabin, examining his grandfather clock with those stunning aquamarine eyes.

And crumpling to the floor right in front of him.

"Whoa." Beau wasn't sure if he'd spoken or not, but he did manage to propel himself out of the doorway and toward the woman who'd just suddenly and unexpectedly clattered to the floor. Pepper barked, and by the time Beau reached her, Ruby hovered over Charlotte in a very protective stance.

"Charlotte?" Beau asked. Then Ruby started licking her face, as if her rough tongue would surely wake her. Beau prayed it would as he took in the unconscious woman now in his kitchen.

"Come on," he said, a hint of desperation in his voice. He had no idea what to do with his hands, where to touch or not touch. "Charlotte? Can you hear me?" He pressed on Ruby's chest to get her to back up.

Pepper barked again, and Beau felt at an utter loss.

Then he remembered he had a phone, and he knew Charlotte's brother. Mason and his family had just moved onto a ranch on the southeast side of Three Rivers, and perhaps he'd know why his younger sister had literally just passed out for no reason.

Chapter Two

Charlotte Wisenhouer could hear someone talking above her. Around her. A male voice seemingly implanted in her eardrums, echoing endlessly.

I'm going to call your brother, okay?

She moaned, because that absolutely couldn't happen. She didn't want Mason and his super-human worrying coming into play here. Everything around her felt squishy and soft as she came back to awareness, and she hated this part of waking up the most.

Because it meant she'd passed out.

She'd lost consciousness enough times in her life to know, and she fought through the clouds in her head for the last memory she possessed. That would give her an idea of where she'd been when her mild heart condition had caused her to faint.

The scent of something male and something canine met her nose. Then alfalfa and maybe dirt. All at once, she remembered—she'd gone inside the cabin where she'd been told to come for her interview.

She'd expected to find someone there waiting for her, but the place had been empty. So she'd left the door slightly ajar and took the liberty at looking at the foreman's pictures. And oh, she knew this foreman.

Beau Peterson. Cowboy god. Tall, dark, and handsome. The star of her teenage dreams.

She'd first met Beau when she was fifteen and he twenty. That was the first time she'd felt the rush of attraction toward the man. But Mason, her overprotective and stern older brother, had told her to stay away from the older cowboy. That he was a player, and he'd only break her heart.

And Charlotte barely had one of those that worked, so she certainly couldn't risk losing pieces of it to men like Beau Peterson.

Her eyelids fluttered open, and she found Beau moving in slow motion as he lifted his phone to his ear. In a swift, desperate movement, her arm flew out and knocked his device away.

He yelped in surprise, and his light brown eyes—or were they hazel? Brownish-hazel?—locked onto hers. "You're awake."

"Don't call my brother."

A few moments passed while Charlotte tried to further ground herself to where she was and what had happened.

"I'm not going to ask if you're okay," Beau said. "But do you want to stand up?" He offered his hand, and Charlotte didn't hesitate to slide hers into it. He helped her sit up, saying,

"Take it easy, now," in that slow, sexy cowboy drawl that always made her cells vibrate in a warm way.

She'd dated men in the past, of course. Not anyone for a while, as she'd grown weary of everyone treating her like she was one breath away from breaking. She'd put nothing of her medical condition on her application here at Three Rivers Ranch, and had she known Beau Peterson was the foreman, she might've worn something a little different for the interview.

As it was, she'd only arrived in town two nights ago, and none of her stuff had been delivered yet. Her luggage had been lost by the airline and not found yet. So she'd borrowed a shirt from her sister-in-law, but unfortunately, Felicity was built like a barrel and most of her clothes came from the men's section.

"You okay, Charlotte?"

The use of her name made her blink and look at Beau again. "You know who I am?"

His smile flickered across his handsome features, making his beard ripple as his cheeks pitched up. "Of course I do," he said. "You came around with Mason plenty of times."

She put her hand on the seat of one of his kitchen chairs and used it to help herself get to her feet. "I didn't meant to trespass. It was just hot outside, and I figured you'd be ready for me."

"That's strange." He straightened and pushed his dogs back.

Charlotte reached out to pat the black lab, who preened under her touch. "Yes, you're so sweet, aren't you?"

"Don't encourage him," Beau said with a dry tone. "He'll never leave you alone."

"And this is the most beautiful collie I've ever seen." She had the classic markings, with intelligent eyes and perked-up ears.

"She just had a bath," Beau said as he flipped on the sink. "I need to shower, but you can hang out with the pups while I do. Shouldn't be long." He washed his hands and grabbed a towel from the stove. "Did you need lunch, or...?"

"Lunch?" Charlotte asked blankly, as if she'd never eaten the meal before. Maybe she shouldn't have looked directly at Beau.

"Yes," he said slowly. "You're an hour early for your interview, Charlotte. I was going to eat lunch, shower, and be ready when you got here." He turned and pulled open the bottom drawer in his fridge. "So I'm going to make pizza. I'll put in extra if you want to eat."

He faced her again, an inquisitive look on his face. "Maybe that's why you fainted? You're hungry?"

Charlotte pressed her lips together, feeling the lies building up inside her. If she didn't speak, was that lying? Could she just nod, indicating her hunger, even if it wasn't true?

She really didn't want to tell him about her heart condition, because she felt a weight getting tied to her lungs. It would drag her down the way it had so many times in the past, and she just wanted to exist on even ground with someone for as long as possible.

"Sure," she managed to choke out. "I didn't realize I was an hour early." And with Three Rivers Ranch forty-five minutes north of town, she couldn't go grab something and be back in time for her interview.

"I can...." She trailed off, not sure what to offer. "Go wait in my car?"

Beau grinned, chuckled, and shook his head. "No, it's fine. We can catch up on Mason while we eat." He busied himself with putting frozen pizza in the oven, and then he nodded down the hall. "I'll be back in a bit. Make yourself at home."

He glanced over to the grandfather clock and the pictures she'd been examining before she fainted. Something crossed his features, but Charlotte couldn't identify it before he turned and walked away from her.

She took a breath and faced the pictures again. The woman in them didn't have her lighter blonde hair, but that hadn't mattered. She'd been show riding, smiling for all she was worth with ribbons and roses, as Charlotte had once.

Before she'd been forced to quit, after she'd fainted while in the saddle. Her family and friends had never treated her the same after that. Once she'd been diagnosed with vasovagal syncope, a mild heart condition that caused her to lose consciousness when her heart rate and blood pressure dropped suddenly.

It almost always happened when she was stressed, in pain, or shocked. Sometimes from standing for too long or not getting enough sleep could trigger the fainting spells too.

It wasn't heart disease, but everyone acted like it was. Like Charlotte was one step away from certain death, of never waking up again.

But she did keep waking up after her fainting spells, which she hadn't had in a while until today. "Which is why you don't want Mason to know," she muttered. She was staying with him and Felicity until she could find a job, and she really wanted to get back to work with horses.

It had been too long, and she gazed at the photos with less fear and surprise and more nostalgia. She'd spent the past fifteen years being a nanny for Mason and Felicity, but their youngest would be in full-day kindergarten next month, and she wasn't needed anymore.

"It's time," she whispered to herself as she turned away from the pictures of who she assumed was Beau's younger sister. She could almost see the shape of his eyes in the pictures, though the woman wore a riding helmet and squinted into the sun.

Behind her, something clicked, and she turned that way. She didn't see Beau, and that would be a lightning-fast shower. Of course, cowboys could do such a thing, and she wasn't surprised the man was bathing during his lunch hour. Sometimes ranch work required that, and he'd been clearly doing something dirty that morning.

She wandered past his kitchen island, both dogs hot on her heels. He didn't keep anything indicating children on the fridge, but he did have a couple of reminders she paused to look at. A ranch Fourth of July picnic at the homestead that had come and gone, and a church potluck breakfast that would happen next weekend.

Not much sat out, though she did spy a couple of coffee mugs in the kitchen sink. This cabin had been equipped with all the kitchen necessities, including a dishwasher and garbage disposal, and a bolt of anticipation drove through Charlotte.

She hadn't lived alone in so long, and she pressed her eyes closed and drew in a long breath of oxygen. If she could get this job here at the ranch, she'd have a cabin like this one to live in. Nothing this big or nice, she was sure, and she'd most likely have a cabinmate.

But she wouldn't be living under the watchful eye of her brother. He wouldn't be making reports about her to their mother. Charlotte, at age thirty-two, would finally be free to strike out and live her own life.

Worry needled through her, but she told herself again, "It's time." She knew everyone around her—all three of her brothers and both of her parents—were worried about her taking on a new job, especially one with horses.

Everyone but Mason lived down in San Antonio, but she still spoke to her mom almost every day. That had been part of the deal when Charlotte had said she was going to make the move north to Three Rivers with Mason and Felicity.

They'd just bought a big ranch on the southeast side of town, and Charlotte had finally graduated from college with a degree in ranch management. She didn't want to be a ranch manager—she wanted to be the Stable Manager here at Three Rivers Ranch.

The position came with a nice salary, as well as a place to live, and Charlotte wanted it as badly as anything she'd wanted before. Everything inside her told her that if she could just get this job, she'd have taken the first step in her quest for independence.

As she started to feel overwhelmed again, Charlotte closed her eyes in an attempt to calm down. "Lord," she whispered. "I need this job. I'm too old to be living with my brother. No one can take care of me forever."

She didn't even want them to. No, it was time for her to take care of herself.

She opened her eyes and caught sight of a long board extending down the hallway. Bowties hung from it, and Charlotte glanced further into the cabin, expecting Beau to return at any moment.

When he didn't, she took a couple of steps to look at the hanging neckwear. A label had been put above it, as well as a picture of a much younger Beau with a cheerful, smiling couple.

Squire and Kelly, the label read, and she took that to mean Beau was standing with the bride and groom—obviously Squire and Kelly.

"Smells like pizza out here."

She spun toward the sound of Beau's voice. He looked at the neat row of labeled bowties, didn't comment on them, and indicated she should go into the kitchen ahead of him. Charlotte practically scurried away from the cowboy, because now he smelled like leather and citrus, soap and spicy cologne.

He followed her into the kitchen, and she wondered if he was dating anyone. If he wasn't, would he ever be interested in someone like her? Someone who had never had a real job, had just barely graduated from college, and really could only get along with horses and family for any length of time.

She'd just have to hide all of that until she had this job and had impressed him with her equine knowledge and skills. Then, and only then, would she think about finding out if Beau had a girlfriend.

The cabin didn't suggest he was married, and he didn't wear any jewelry on his left hand either.

"So," he said as he slid a tray of cooked pizza onto the stovetop. "Talk to me about being a Stable Manager."

Charlotte had not anticipated such a statement, and her mind went blank. "That's not even a question," she said.

He grinned at her and opened a drawer. As he rifled through it to find something, he said, "I don't have a set of questions. I want to know what you think being a Stable Manger is."

"The Stable Manger manages the stable," she said.

Beau chuckled and shook his head as he cut the pizza into triangles. "Walked right into that one, didn't I?"

She finally allowed a smile to touch her face too. Charlotte was ready for this job. This interview. All of it. As Beau got out plates and started putting pizza slices on them, her phone chimed.

With Mason's special *ding-a-ling-zing!*

Her heartbeat nearly fell out of her chest, and Charlotte's vision turned white for a half-second. Then she lifted her phone to read his text.

Beau already called me? What's going on?

Nothing, she tapped out quickly. A plate of food slid toward her on the counter, and she glanced at it long enough to make sure it wouldn't fall to the floor. She needed to keep her heartbeat pumping and her stress level low, or she might pass out again.

Then she wouldn't be able to blame her earlier episode on being hungry.

But Mason had just texted again. Three times.

Zing, zing, zing.

You better tell him about your heart condition.

Or I might have to.

I won't lie if he asks me, Char. Just tell him, okay? It'll be fine.

But she had no idea how to do that, and when he asked, "Everything okay?" she shoved her phone in her back pocket and pulled the barstool out.

"Yes," she said. "Just telling Mace I messed up the time of the interview, and he says it'll be fine." She gave Beau her best smile, her heartbeat betraying her *again* by thumping and bumping when he returned it with a gorgeous grin of his own.

She couldn't tell him. Could she?

The war continued silently inside her as she lifted her pizza to her mouth and took a big bite. She hadn't eaten, and she certainly didn't need to add hunger to the issues she currently had.

"So, tell me why you want this job," Beau said between bites. "And what you've been doing up till now."

In that moment, Charlotte realized no matter what job she applied for or where she went, she was going to have to disclose about her health. Why else would she have taken over a decade to graduate from college? Why else would she have lived with either her parents or her brother until she was well over thirty years old?

Her head felt too heavy for her neck to hold up, and then she remembered who she was. Charlotte Wisenhouer. A daughter, aunt, and friend. She had a Father in Heaven who loved her and had led her here.

She'd fought for every single thing she'd achieved in her life, and she'd done it with a weaker heart than others.

She could get this job without telling Beau. And she could keep it once he knew.

So she took a breath, called on the Lord to give her the right words, and looked at Beau before she started to answer.

Chapter Three

"I was looking at those pictures over on the sideboard," Charlotte said, which didn't answer anything Beau had asked her. "Is she your sister?"

"Yes," he said, noting the cautious tone in his own voice. "One of them. Her name is Dolly."

"I used to show horses," Charlotte said, her pretty little voice making Beau want to lean closer and have her tell him more about that. But that was the flirty version of himself. This version was conducting an interview, and he wasn't going to step outside those bounds.

Part of him realized that he couldn't hire Charlotte. If he did, she'd live and work here, and that always made dating someone more complicated. Beau didn't want complicated, not in his love life. Not in anything, but especially when it came to women.

Beau had learned he was a simple cowboy, and he just wanted something simple. A beautiful wife to come home to after he'd thrown moldy hay out of a loft for too many hours. An easy conversation about their big dreams, vacations they'd never take, and horses.

"I love horses," Charlotte said next, as if reading his thoughts. "Some people are afraid of them, but that's only because they can't really speak their language. I can."

"A-ha. So that'll make you a good stable manager."

"It will," she said. "The listing said you had forty-plus horses here. When I was showing horses, I worked at a boarding barn. Hundreds of horses. I can easily care for forty."

"Plus," he said. "We share equines with Courage Reins, though they have some facilities of their own, usually for horses they're putting through training."

"I simply get along with horses," Charlotte said. "And I love talking to them. Mucking out their stalls. Feeding them and giving them treats. Watching them run along the fence when they don't get to go on trail rides."

A wide smile covered her whole face. "I wasn't the Stable Manager at the last barn where I worked, but I can do the job no problem."

"What was your last job?" Beau asked. "I glanced over your résumé this morning, but I don't recall."

"I, uh." Charlotte cleared her throat, which only drew Beau's attention to her. She put off the scent of fresh cotton, and she held her pizza in the cutest way possible. "I've been a nanny for Mason's kids." She took a huge bite of her lunch then, and Beau grinned.

Why, he wasn't sure. Only that she seemed uncomfortable talking about her previous job—which had nothing to do with horses, he noted—and thought a giant bite of pizza would save her from having to speak more about this topic. "Is that right?" he asked. "How many kids they got?"

She chewed quickly now, and Beau thought she'd certainly scrape her throat she swallowed so fast. "Four," she said. "The youngest is moving into kindergarten this year, so they don't need a nanny anymore."

"Thus, you need a job."

"It would be nice to have a place of my own too," she said. "I've been living with them for...a while."

Beau wanted to ask how long, because it seemed to be a thing for Charlotte. Instead, he nodded and asked, "Do they have horses?"

"No, sir," she said. "Two dogs, though. Same as you."

"So he moves up here to a new ranch, and you came with?"

Watching her squirm shouldn't bring him so much joy. Or make him want to flirt even more obviously with her. "So you're in touch with him," she said.

"When someone buys a ranch worth over a million dollars, word gets around," Beau said casually.

"They sold a big place outside of Austin."

"Heard that too," Beau said.

"I needed a change of scenery," she said.

"Where are your parents?"

Charlotte folded the end of her pizza and shoved the whole thing into her mouth. Beau couldn't help it then; he laughed. She simply gaped at him with wide eyes, and through his chuckles, he said, "At least I know your tell now."

"What?" she asked around the pizza. Somehow, he even found that attractive.

Beau told himself to get control of his hormones. He simply hadn't had a woman in his cabin in a long time. Especially not one as pretty as Charlotte.

He shook the thought from his head. "When you don't want to talk, you take a big bite."

She covered her mouth with her hand as she swallowed. "That is not true."

"Then where are your parents?" He threw up a prayer that they hadn't died. He'd been good enough friends with Mason that he'd like to think if one of his parents had died, Beau would've gotten a phone call.

"My folks and other brothers are in San Antonio," she said. "I didn't want to go back there."

"Why not?"

"Felt like moving backward," she said, her gaze darting all over his kitchen. Ah, another tell. Something about San Antonio plagued her, but Beau told himself he didn't have to know all the answers today.

And that was him thinking he'd get to see Charlotte again, and he didn't even know if that was true. So he backpedaled and reached to tap awake his phone. He'd compiled a list of questions for that afternoon's interviews, and he caught sight of one.

"Have you ever worked in management before?"

"Yes," she said without missing a beat.

"How so?" He looked at her. "Before the nannying?"

"No, inside the nannying. You try getting four kids out the door for school when they start at different times, everyone wants something different for breakfast, and half the children can't find their shoes." She cocked her eyebrows at him, and Beau had exactly zero experience with children, so he couldn't argue.

He'd known plenty of kids over the years, but he hadn't taken care of any of them for longer than ten minutes, so he said, "Fair enough. What other qualities do you have that would be good for a Stable Manager?"

"I'm detail-oriented," she said. "So I'll set a schedule with those equines, and they'll love me for it. I'm an early riser, so you'll never have to wonder if breakfast will be on time. I love to ride as much as I like brushing down the horses, cleaning tack, and dressing wounds, so the horses will never be bored, wounded, hurt, alone, or dirty."

"No one ever wants a dirty horse." Beau gave her a smile she did not return.

"I'm sure you're joking," she said. "Because no, once horses are done with their work, they should be treated right, and that includes proper hygiene."

"Horse hygiene," he said.

"Exactly." She picked up her second slice of pizza and took a normal-sized bite. She possessed confidence when talking about horses, that was for sure.

Beau polished off his third piece and dusted his hands. "Okay, Miss Wisenhouer," he said. "I have four more inter-views this afternoon. I'll call you soon, okay?"

Her face fell, but she nodded. After she swallowed, she said, "Yes, sir." It didn't take long after that for her to help him clean up by putting her plate in the sink and heading out. Beau waved to her from the front door, everything inside him wanting to ask her to dinner.

But he didn't, and he wouldn't. Maybe if he met someone better than her for the job that afternoon, when he called and broke the bad news, he could ask her out then. "And if she's the best person for the job?" he asked himself as Charlotte disappeared between the barn and the stable. A parking lot sat on the other side of the structures, and she'd surely parked there.

Beau went back inside the house, and he quickly texted the other four applicants about a change of venue for the interviews. He could do them in the conference room at the administration building.

That way, the soft, feminine scent of Charlotte's skin wouldn't get erased as quickly from his cabin.

* * *

About quitting time, Beau knocked on Squire Ackerman's door. It stood open, and the owner of the ranch glanced up from his laptop. "Yep, Beau."

"I think I've found us a great Stable Manager."

Squire leaned back in his chair and stretched his arms above his head. He yawned, and Beau reminded himself that he wasn't that much younger than Squire. His oldest had already completed a year at Baylor University, and Beau would never quite measure up to the other cowboy.

"Come in," he said.

Beau stayed leaning against the doorjamb, a folder in his hand. "They'll be great," he said.

"A great new Stable Manager," Squire said. "Why do you look like you've swallowed bees then?"

Beau cracked a smile then. He pushed away from the wall and sauntered over to Squire's desk. He heaved a sigh as he sat down. "She's perfect for it. Her brother swears by her ability with horses, though she hasn't done much with them in recent years."

He tossed the folder containing Charlotte's résumé onto the desk. "But I figure that's not a bad thing. She won't have any preconceived ways of doing things. She'll manage it the way you and Pete want."

"The way *you* want," Squire corrected.

"Sure," Beau said easily. "Have you been hearin' the pronoun I'm using?" He flipped open the folder. "It's a woman."

Squire glanced at the pages inside, but he didn't' read them. "Okay," he said.

"Our female cabin is full." Beau raised his right eyebrow at Squire. "Three of 'em in there, and there's no way we can cram in a fourth."

Squire sighed, though his expression danced with a hint of light. "And the rest of the cabins are full too." He looked up to the ceiling, as if the answers would be there—or God would send him a solution from heaven.

Beau swallowed, his nerves firing at him. "All but mine, boss."

Squire's eyes yanked back to his. "You're the foreman."

"The position comes with boarding," he said. "I've got three bedrooms, boss. I can share. I've—"

"You're the foreman," Squire said again.

"But I'm not married. I have no family." Beau hunched down in his chair. "It's ridiculous I have that big cabin anyway."

"So we'll move two men in with you, so this...." He peered at the paper in the folder. "Charlotte can have her own place?"

"About," Beau said.

"Who would you move?"

Beau let his chest puff up as he breathed in. "Thus why I knocked on your door."

"We just rearranged everyone," Squire said. "To find the pairings that get along. So we'll move a whole pairing, but...."

Beau let his boss work through the other men who worked the ranch. Three Rivers had eleven cowboy cabins, including his, in a row leading from the homestead to the administration building, and they were full.

All full up.

Eighteen men and three women, plus Beau, worked the ranch. Plus Squire and his family. Peter Marshall and his wife owned Courage Reins, and he employed a bunch of people who didn't live out here on the ranch.

Brynn and Ethan Greene owned Bowman's Breeds, a horse training facility down on the same side as the homestead. They maintained a residence in town as well, and sometimes the cowboys who worked at Three Rivers had to head over to her place to tend to her horses.

Beau had always been happy to do it, because that was what cowboys did. They helped each other when necessary.

"There is not a pairing we can move as-is that you won't want to kill within a week." Squire leaned forward, his smile slow and his expression challenging. "Is that about where you landed?"

"Yep," Beau said.

"So what are you going to do?"

"I would like you to tell me what to do."

Squire gave him a long look and picked up the folder. "She's it, huh?"

"Better than the other four who applied."

He read through the paper and said nothing. Finally, he closed it, his movements slow. "You've got three bedrooms and two baths, right?"

"Right."

"And a loft."

"Yes, sir."

Squire tossed the folder down on the desk. "Seems like enough room for you and Miss Wisen—whatever."

Beau smiled at him and said, "Wisenhouer."

"Make the call. See what she says. No matter what, someone's gonna have to move in with you, and I don't see the sense in making two men move—one of whom you only deal with when absolutely necessary—when she can just take one of the bedrooms."

Beau picked up the folder. "Okay, boss." He got to his feet and turned toward the door.

"Is that what you were thinking?" Squire asked.

"Yes," Beau said. "But it sounded crazy in my thoughts, so I wasn't sure." He turned back at the doorway. "Thanks, Squire."

"Do you think she'll agree to it?"

"I have no idea," Beau said. "I don't know her."

"Mm, you will soon enough."

Beau tipped his hat at Squire, who grinned him right out of the office. He could make the phone call from the admin building, but instead, Beau made the quick trip home. He wasn't sure how to say what needed to be said, so he fed his dogs and took another frozen meal out and got it cooking in the oven.

He showered. He wandered over to the grandfather clock and the pictures on the sideboard. "Dolly and her horses," he murmured to himself.

Time passed, and he ate dinner without making the phone call. His bedtime approached, and he'd told everyone he'd let them know that evening. This job definitely had things about it he didn't like, but for the most part, Beau loved being the foreman.

He made four quick phone calls to deliver bad news to the applicants who hadn't gotten the job. The grandfather clock chimed eight times, and Beau exhaled heavily.

"Just do it," he said, and he grabbed Charlotte's folder so he could get her phone number. One more phone call, and he could rest easy.

He tapped in the numbers, his fingers moving slower and

slower. "It's a phone call," he coached himself as he stared at the green button. "It's only a phone call."

Beau touched his screen to make the call, every cell in his body vibrating as if they were each experiencing an individual earthquake.

Chapter Four

Charlotte held up four miniature ice cream sandwiches, two in each hand, and called, "Who wants ice cream?"

It was no wonder she was the favorite aunt. Her three nieces and her one nephew all started clamoring for the treat, which their mother had approved.

"I'm the oldest," Ella said. "I should get one first."

Charlotte grinned at her, and she did get the first one. Not because she was the oldest, but because she stood the tallest. Charlotte could easily hand her the treat over the heads of the other kids, and then she presented an ice cream sandwich to Kennedy, the cutest seven-year-old on the planet.

Garrett got his next, and then Charlotte sat down and pulled the youngest onto her lap before she passed over the ice cream. "There you go, Alice."

"Thank you, Char-Char."

She had to help Alice get the wrapper off, and once she'd done that, Charlotte couldn't help looking over to the clock.

Eight-ten. Was Beau ever going to call? She wasn't sure if no news was good news or not. Surely he wasn't still interviewing, but she really had no idea what the hiring process was like at Three Rivers Ranch.

She'd put a show on for the kids while Mason and Felicity packed lunches for their picnic tomorrow. But really, she just wanted her phone to ring. She'd avoided Mason after returning to his ranch, which sat over an hour from Three Rivers. She didn't want to answer his questions, and she hadn't thought of a reason why Beau would've called Mason other than her health problems.

So she'd looked through the job boards, just to have a back-up plan if she didn't get the Stable Manager position. She'd helped with dinner, and she'd thanked the Good Lord above that Mason had been distracted with a portion of the shed's roof that had come off in the wind.

Now, the kids finished their ice cream, and Beau still hadn't called. Charlotte had half a mind to go into the kitchen and demand Mason give her his number. She'd call him herself if he wasn't going to tell her about the job tonight.

Just when her desperation had started to choke her, her phone rang. She nearly threw Alice off her lap in her hurry to get the device out of her pocket. "Please, Lord," she begged when she saw the number didn't belong to anyone she had saved in her phone. "Let this be Beau."

"Who's Beau?" Garrett asked.

"No one," she said, which was about as far from the truth as possible. If he was no one, why had she been thinking about him all day? And not only about the job and potentially working for him.

It seemed like all her fifteen-year-old fantasies had only been lying dormant, and the human memory was a very powerful thing. It had conjured up everything she'd once felt for him, but in a new, more mature way.

She tapped on the call. "Hello?"

"Miss Wisenhouer?"

She knew Beau's voice instantly. Relief rushed through her. "I have been waiting for you to call," she said. "You've been driving me nuts."

He chuckled in that deep, throaty, rich voice that tickled her attraction. "Sorry, Miss Wisenhouer."

"You don't need to call me that."

"Oh? So a first-name basis is okay?"

Charlotte took a moment, because it sure seemed like he was flirting with her. *Flirting*. "Yes," she said. "In fact, sometimes I'm called Char or even Char-Char."

He laughed, the sound delicious and robust. "I don't think I'll be using that last one."

She grinned too, and she paced down the hall toward the bedrooms. "So? What's the news?" *Please let it be good*, she prayed. *Please, please, please.*

Beau cleared his throat, which so wasn't good. Charlotte pressed her eyes closed and tried to will her pulse to stay steady. She didn't need to get all excited, or depressed, or worried, or scared before he'd even said anything.

But clearing his throat? Never a good sign.

Maybe he's getting a cold, she thought.

"Let me explain," Beau said.

"That doesn't sound good."

"Depends on your definition of that word."

"Go on then."

"I want you as the Stable Manager. You're the best candidate, and I think you'd do a real good job."

Charlotte let his words sink into her ears, and as they did, she grinned and grinned. "All right," she said. "I accept."

"You didn't let me explain."

"What's to explain?" She couldn't even imagine moving onto that ranch. Into a place of her own. Of course, she'd have to share with someone. Maybe two people. But it wouldn't be her brother and sister-in-law.

"Charlotte, we're full-up here at Three Rivers."

She took a breath, her mouth opening to say something. But what, she didn't know. A puff of air came out of her mouth, and she promptly closed it again.

"We have three cowgirls here," he said. "Their cabin is full. We just went through this whole restructuring—you know what? None of this is important. Here's the situation: You got the job, but if you take it, you'll have to live with me."

Silence flooded the line. "Live...with you." She wasn't asking. She was simply trying to make the words understandable.

"Yes." Beau cleared his throat again. "The foreman's cabin is bigger than the others. I currently live alone, and I have three bedrooms, two baths, and a loft. I talked to Squire, and we figure it's enough room for the two of us."

"The two of us."

"You can think on it," he said. "Talk to your brother. Your mama. Whatever. Whoever. I can show you the cabin and you can pick either of the two empty bedrooms. We'd each have our own bathroom, but yours isn't in your room. We'll obviously have to share the kitchen and living room, but we could set you up in the loft with a TV room or whatever. I'm—well, I'm going to stop talking now and let you have a chance."

"I—well, to be honest, I don't know what to say."

"Think about it," he said. "Come back out tomorrow if you want to see the cabin. I'm around, and I can run over to the cabin anytime."

Charlotte turned around and looked back down the hall toward the living room. "I—what about lunch again? What if I brought it for the two of us?"

Beau let several seconds go by. "Like a date?"

"A date?"

"Forget it," Beau said quickly. "Yes, absolutely. Bring lunch, and I'll show you the cabin."

"All right," ghosted out of Charlotte's mouth.

"You've got my number?" he asked. "Call me when you get here."

"Okay."

"Okay," he repeated, his voice brusque and business-like now. "Great. Good-bye." He hung up, and Charlotte stood there, staring at the wall.

"Live with him," she repeated. "Like a date?" She flew into gear then, her breath hitching as she ran down the hall and into the kitchen. "Felicity."

Her sister-in-law had finished packing their picnic lunch

for tomorrow's outing, and Charlotte had no idea where she'd gone. The summer evening sunshine still leant plenty of light to the day, and she hurried out onto the deck.

Felicity sat there with a glass of sweet tea, both dogs, and Mason. She looked up and immediately set her tea down. "My goodness, Charlotte. What's wrong?"

Charlotte froze, not wanting to talk about this in front of Mason. But he'd seen her too, and he actually got to his feet. "You're going to pass out," he said. "Come sit down."

"I'm fine," she said, though she did feel a bit lightheaded.

Her brother moved her to his chair and loomed over her. "What's going on? Did you get the job?"

She nodded, a certain numbness spreading through her. "I got it."

"That's great news, honey," Felicity said, and she patted Charlotte's arm. She'd been nothing but kind to Charlotte all these years, and Charlotte loved her nieces and nephew. They all had a hint of red in their hair which came from Felicity, as well as their super Southern streak, as she hailed from Alabama.

"Don't get all worked up about it," she said. "This is good news."

"Yes." Charlotte looked at her, suddenly seeing everything. "I won't be living with you guys anymore."

"Is that what you're worried about?" Mason sat down on the end of the lounge chair. "Char, you wanted this."

"I know," she said. "I'm just saying—that's not what I'm saying. I'm not upset about it." She gave her light-haired brother a glare. He shot it right back at her. "I'm saying, I got the job, and I'm taking it."

She didn't need to discuss living with Beau Peterson with anyone, least of all her older brother who'd once told her to stop making moon eyes at the cowboy. *He's nothing but a flirt, Char. Stay away from him.*

As a fifteen-year-old, she'd listened to her brother. Not that she and Beau had ever had much opportunity to be around one another.

They did now—and Mason had absolutely no say in it.

"It comes with a cabin," she said. "I'm—" She couldn't speak through her sudden smile. She started to laugh, a hint of mania accompanying the rush of emotions streaming through her. "You guys know I love you, right?"

Tears filled her eyes, and she simply couldn't feel this much and not have a release. "I'm going to miss you and the kids terribly, but I'm—I'm ready for this." She reached out and grabbed onto Mason's hand. "I can do this."

"I never said you couldn't."

"You act like it." She released his hand and brushed at her tears.

Felicity wiped at her own face. "You're going to be brilliant, baby." She smiled and smiled. "Tell her, Mace."

"You're going to be brilliant, Char," he said dutifully. He did smile at her, and the overprotective brother melted away for just a moment. "Just make sure you don't overdo it."

And there he was again. Bossy. Overbearing. Always right.

"I'm going out there again tomorrow," she said, the tears

finally subsiding. "I'll get everything worked out, when I'll move and all that."

"And did you talk about a signal or safe word for when you're not feeling well?" Mason asked.

"Not yet," she hedged, and that wasn't a lie. She'd stabilized quickly after sitting down, after the rush of everything. "Oh, I'm so excited. I'm going to go tell the kids, and then I'm gonna call Momma."

She got back to her feet and headed inside the house. What were the chances that Mason, Felicity, or her mother would ever come to the foreman's cabin on Three Rivers Ranch? A place forty-five minutes from anything?

"Slim to none," she muttered to herself, the three words making her giddier than ever. She could pack everything she owned into her SUV, no problem. She didn't need Mason's help with furniture or heavy items. She'd been living with them for ages, and it was assumed the cabin would come furnished.

No problem. Nothing to explain. She wasn't lying if no one asked. So no one needed to know she was *living* with her boss.

No one needed to know that at all.

Chapter Five

Beau pulled up to the white-sided farmhouse on the quiet street in one of the small communities in Three Rivers. He could feel the life pouring from the house, and it almost kept him from getting out of his truck and going inside.

He did so anyway, calling as he entered, "Howdy-ho, Garth. It's just me."

"We're in the sunroom."

"Of course they are," he muttered to himself. Garth Ahlstrom had run the ranch as the foreman for the past couple of decades—maybe not that long—and he'd retired a little over six months ago.

Beau had gotten the foreman job after him, and he lived in the same cabin where Garth and Juliette had raised their two boys. They weren't quite adults yet, and Beau wasn't sure if he'd find the teens in the sunroom.

He knew he'd find Garth and Juliette, and he grinned at

them as he entered the golden-lit room at the back of the house. "It's warm here," he said.

"We turn the fans on in the afternoon." Garth looked up at him from the wood and knife in his hand. He'd been carving for as long as Beau had known him, and Garth claimed he needed something for his hands to do so his mind didn't run away from him. "What brings you by?"

Beau groaned as he sat down in an available chair. "Nothing. Where are the boys?"

"Football camp," Juliette said with a smile. Her hair had started to go gray, but she was still soft and wonderful, and Beau had never met anyone as good with animals as her. Maybe Squire, who did work as the full-time veterinarian on the ranch, and Juliette had been the vet technician.

"You have business in town?" Garth asked.

Beau nodded and clasped his hands between his knees. "Yeah, yep." He took another breath. "Had some pick-ups at the feed store. Grabbed some breakfast." He raised his head and looked over to his friends. "Prepping the cabin for someone to move in this weekend."

Garth's eyebrows lifted right up to his already-gray hair. "Someone's moving in with you?"

"The other cabins are full," he said.

"You're the foreman." Garth exchanged a glance with his wife. "Who is it? Why are they moving in?"

"Johnny went back to Tennessee," Beau said. "We need a new Stable Manager, and since Three Rivers is a drive and a half from everything, we decided to list it with board."

"Ah."

"I didn't anticipate hiring a woman." Beau let the words sit there as he looked out the screens and into the backyard. "Pond looks good."

"It's a woman?" Juliette asked. "You're moving in with a woman?"

"She's technically moving in with me." Beau's chest tightened slightly, but he'd had a few days to get used to the idea of Charlotte living in his cabin. She'd been out to the ranch twice since. First to look through the cabin and accept the job. He'd given her the paperwork and all that.

Then, she'd come yesterday to pick a bedroom and take some measurements. She'd turned in her paperwork, and she'd be moving in tomorrow.

Tomorrow.

Beau could barely believe it, and he'd come here expressly to tell Garth about this and see what he said.

"Who is she?" Garth asked, his voice the forced casual that said he was working through some surprise before saying too much.

"I actually know her," Beau said. His shoulders rippled as he did a wavy shrug. "I mean, kind of. I know her brother. Mason and I were college roommates for that one year I went to school."

Neither Garth nor Juliette said anything, and Beau looked over to them. "I met Charlotte—she's about seven or eight years younger than Mason—when I first came to Three Rivers. He interviewed there too."

"Before my time," Garth said.

"Barely," Beau said. "He met his wife, and they settled on

a ranch down in the Hill Country. They've sold it now, and they bought the Lucas Ranch."

"Oh, boy," Juliette said, her eyebrows going up now. "That's a nice place."

Yes, it was. Beau simply nodded, though the differences between his life and Mason's stood out like black ink on snowy white paper.

"She comes with good endorsements," Beau said. "Used to show horses." He didn't say anything about the vibrating in his chest whenever he pictured her in his mind, or how his fingers tingled even now to touch her hair.

"Anyway, she's coming tomorrow. In true Kelly Ackerman fashion, I'm catering lunch for anyone who comes to help."

"Great," Garth said. "Me and the boys like free lunch."

"The boys have football camp tomorrow," Juliette said.

"Then just me." He grinned past his wife to Beau. "What else aren't you sayin'?"

His first instinct was to say *nothing* again. But he trusted Garth explicitly, and Beau had never been one to hold his words too deeply inside. "I maybe think she's real pretty," he said, his mouth suddenly made of glue and sand. "If I'd met her anywhere else, I'd probably ask her out."

"Oh, boy," Juliette said again.

Garth simply stared at him, his grumpy foreman cowboy face etched into his skin. Beau had seen it so often over the years, he could draw it from memory. He glared, then blinked, then looked out into the yard too.

Beau followed his gaze, his lungs stuffed with too much air.

He tried to blow it all out, but it wouldn't go. Plus, he just had to breathe in more.

"Then ask her out," Garth finally said. "You deserve to be happy too, and maybe it'll be with her."

"Maybe," Beau said. He didn't feel the need to spill about how he'd already said the word "date" to Charlotte. She'd said nothing of it when she'd brought meatball subs and sweet pea salad, and they'd eaten, gone over the contract, and then walked through the cabin.

She'd worn shiny lip gloss on her mouth, and it had followed Beau into his dreams that night—and every night since.

"I'm—she's going to be right across the hall. If it's going to be a thing, I'll know soon enough."

"Yep," Garth said. "What time?"

"She said she and Mason would be there around nine."

"So you have time to do your morning live."

"Yes," Beau said. "Did you see it this morning?"

"Beautiful sunrise," Garth said. "And the baby goats were a nice touch." He smiled over to Beau again, who should probably look at the comments on his livestream from that morning. He realized he'd have to tell Charlotte about it, and he took out his phone to add it to the list of things they needed to talk about.

Towels. Laundry day. Food. The air conditioner.

And now, the live stream he did every morning under the social media handle Sunrise Cowboy. He had hundreds of followers who joined him for coffee and calmness to watch the sunrise and talk about the cowboy way of life, cattle ranching, and more, and Beau wouldn't want Charlotte disrupting his filming.

"I better go," he said. "I've got heaps of work on the ranch today, and then I've got to clean out a bedroom tonight."

"This is a big weekend for you," Garth said. "Move-in on Saturday. Wedding on Sunday."

Beau had very nearly forgotten about the wedding. With a jolt, he said, "Yeah," as he got to his feet. "See you tomorrow. Or don't come. We'll have lots of help."

"See you tomorrow," Garth said, and Beau wouldn't be surprised if he found Garth in his kitchen at daybreak, a thermos of coffee he could drink during the live stream.

As Beau left, he looked up into the cloudless blue sky, the air so hot he almost held his breath as he hurried to his truck. "Thank you for good friends to calm me," he murmured to himself as he got behind the wheel.

He did feel calmer now, and in seventy-two hours, the weekend would be over—and Beau would have two major things behind him.

Only seventy-two hours to go.

* * *

"What are you doing with that?" Bennett asked as Beau took down one end of the bowtie display.

"I think just storing it in my closet," Beau said. "Grab that end and lift it off the nail."

Bennett did, and then Beau moved down the length of it until he could hold it without one end dropping to the floor.

"Probably a good idea," Bennett said. "Lots of questions around the bowties."

"She's seen them," Beau said. "But, it's...." He didn't know how to finish the sentence, so he simply took the bowties he'd worn to all the cowboy weddings over the years into his room and stood the board up on its end in the corner of his closet.

"Does the desk stay?" Peter Marshall stuck his head into Beau's bedroom. "Maybe she'd like a desk in her room."

"We can leave it for now," Beau said. "I don't know what she has." He moved to follow his friend into the bedroom across the hall from his, where he'd kept his gym equipment and a desktop computer. Some storage bins had been stacked in the closet. Old memorabilia from high school leaned up against the wall.

At least it had.

Now, almost everything had been cleared away. Beau had either moved it into the third bedroom, which he would continue to use, or gotten rid of it. He'd thought about putting it in the loft, but he wanted to offer that space to Charlotte. Perhaps she'd like a small office or place to escape all her own.

Beau's nerves felt frayed, like someone had taken a pair of scissors and run them along the length of his cells, trying to curl them into ribbons. Everything felt too short, shabby, and in need of a good scrub.

"I've got the curtains," Kelly said, and Beau moved out of the way. "Finn's here with the vacuum too."

"Great," Beau said. "Thanks, Kelly." She went past him and over to the window, where Garth and Pete helped her hang a rod for the curtains for Charlotte's bedroom.

"Towels, toiletries, and toilet paper," someone bellowed from out in the cabin, and Beau went to thank Squire for bringing in extra items ahead of time.

"Going okay?" Squire asked as he passed over a fresh stack of towels.

Beau took them and opened the linen closet behind the door in the bathroom Charlotte would use. "Yeah," he said. "The room's cleaned out. Mostly. Finn's going to vacuum it. They're hanging curtains now. We left the desk, and all we have to do is load the bed."

The ranch had bought a new queen-sized mattress for the cabin, as they didn't have extra bedrooms or furniture at the moment.

"Kel had the sheets and stuff," Squire said.

"Okay." Beau put the toilet paper under the bathroom sink, and Squire arranged the shampoo, conditioner, and soap on the counter.

"You okay on dishes?" Squire asked.

"Yeah," Beau said. "All that's fine." He honestly didn't know what Charlotte would need. The contract included a place to live, and that came with furniture—a bed, couches, dining room table and chairs—and the ranch had upheld their end of that.

Charlotte wouldn't need any furniture at all, and she'd texted that she didn't "have much," she was bringing with her tomorrow. That sounded like a subjective thing, and Beau was simply trying to be prepared.

He knew she hadn't been living in a place of her own, so

he wanted to supply things like towels that she might not bring with her. It was a long way to town, after all.

Beau left the bathroom and called, "We're bringing in the bed."

"Finn's almost done vacuuming," Pete said as he came out of the bedroom. "Let's get it."

They loaded the frame, boxed springs, and mattress into the bedroom, and Kelly took over dressing it. Only minutes later, those who'd come to help him prep this room crowded into the doorway and looked at the bedroom.

"It's perfect," Kelly said.

"Not bad," Beau admitted. He refrained from asking the others if they found this strange in any way. It had been decided.

His phone chirped, and he pulled it out to look at it. "It's Charlotte." He scanned the text quickly. "She's bringing her brother with her in the morning. Says it's his truck and her SUV, so not much."

She'd sent a picture, and while it didn't look like much, her boxes and bags had filled two vehicles. "She wants to know if there will be help here."

"Yep," Bennett said. "Plenty for that."

"We're doing a ranch wide luncheon," Kelly said, and Beau very nearly dropped his phone.

"What? No, we don't need to do that."

Squire started to laugh. "Have you met my wife?" He clapped Beau on the shoulder. "Hey, think of it this way. You won't have to clean up after anyone here."

With that, everyone started filing out of the house. Beau

followed them, saying good-bye and thank you in rapid succession until only he remained in the cabin. Charlotte hadn't moved in yet, but something about the place felt different.

Maybe because it wasn't entirely his anymore.

He breathed out, and went to find something to eat for dinner that night. "Charlotte will be here in the morning," he told himself. "And Mason too."

Beau wondered if his friend would lecture him about dating Charlotte, and then he wondered what he'd do if Mason did.

"Guess we'll find out tomorrow," he said, and since he rose early, made coffee, and had to get his phone set up for the sunrise, he went to bed.

Now, if only sleep would claim him, he wouldn't be playing and then replaying how tomorrow's move-in might go.

Chapter Six

Charlotte frowned as her brother's dust rose up on the dirt road they drove down. Everything about Mason had been annoying her for the past few days. He'd insisted on accompanying her out to Three Rivers Ranch, though she'd told him repeatedly she didn't need his help.

In the end, she'd have had to make two trips to get everything she owned out to the cabin, or she'd have to rent a truck. She didn't want to do either, so she'd let Mason help by filling the bed of his truck with her things.

She wished she'd led the way out here, so she didn't have to drive in his choking dust. Beau had told her how to get past the barns and stables so she could park behind the administration building and closer to the cabin.

Charlotte refused to call it his cabin or the foreman's cabin. She was going to live there too. It could easily be labeled as *her* cabin. Of course, it really wasn't, but Charlotte needed something to cling to so she could get through the next couple of hours.

Moving in. Unpacking. Lunch with everyone on the ranch. Beau had texted her early this morning to say Squire and Kelly Ackerman had decided to host a luncheon down the lane at the homestead for everyone on the ranch that day.

"You'll be part of this ranch family," she told herself. "After this morning." She wasn't sure she wanted to jump right in with both feet, but she also didn't see how she had a choice.

She trundled along behind her brother, and she waited while he backed the truck up to the cabin. She got out of her SUV and let him do the same with her car, so she could just open the back and start to take things out of it.

"Morning," Beau said, and Charlotte spun toward the sexy sound of his voice.

Her pulse bobbed in her throat, but he made everything run faster through her instead of slowing them down. So she didn't feel like running or fainting. No, she wanted to stay right beside him and bathe in the warmth coming from his smile, from his skin, from his spirit.

"Good morning," she said pleasantly. "It's—here." She gestured to the SUV as the back opened.

"Won't take but ten minutes," Beau said almost like it was a promise, and Charlotte watched as more cowboys came around the corner of his cabin. Without any instructions at all, they started picking up her totes, her boxes, her bags, and taking them inside.

"Beau." Mason laughed heartily and grabbed onto the cowboy Charlotte couldn't look away from. She'd ignored what he'd said about their lunch earlier this week being a date, but now she couldn't stop thinking about what going out with him would actually be like.

"Mason." Both cowboys laughed now, and they embraced as they did. "You're lookin' good."

"So are you, brother." Mason sized him up from boot to hat, and then he glanced over to Charlotte. His smile faltered slightly, and she wondered what expression she wore on her face. Mason had always had a special way of seeing right through her, even when she tried to hide things from him. So Charlotte ducked her head and moved toward the SUV.

She retrieved her purse and her backpack with her laptop, her eReader, and her chargers, and she headed into the cabin. It smelled like candy and roses, and she hadn't experienced that before. Beau had definitely been sprucing this place up for her arrival.

The thought made her warm and smiley, and she put her purse and backpack on the dining room table. The décor hadn't changed that much, but she did noticed the row of bowties had disappeared, and that most of the feminine scent came from the bathroom she was claiming as hers.

She smiled at the neatly hung towels waiting for her, and the bottles of plumeria-scented soaps and shampoos sitting on the counter.

"It's okay?" Beau asked as his tall, broad frame filled the doorway.

"It's perfect," she said. "Thank you, Beau."

"Close quarters," Mason said, and Beau shifted so Charlotte could see him. He didn't wear the same sparkles and rainbows she felt shining in her veins.

"Mason," she warned. "I don't want to hear it."

Beau looked between her and him. "I do. What's going on?"

"You're living with my sister," Mason said. "That's what's going on." He folded his arms, and Charlotte had never felt so trapped. She couldn't get out of the long, narrow bathroom without bursting through the two cowboys, which she wasn't going to do.

"Did you know she tried to keep the living conditions a secret?" Mason asked.

Beau cocked his eyebrows at Charlotte without meeting her eyes fully. Before he could answer Mason's question, she said, "I'm thirty-two years old," she said. "You're not my keeper."

"Char—"

"I have it handled, Mason. This is none of your business. *You* don't have to live here. *I* do."

Mason glared at her, his blue-green eyes burning like angry flames. Without looking away from her, he thumped Beau's chest. "Keep an eye on her, Beau." Then he swung the full weight of his overprotective brother gaze on Beau.

Charlotte wanted to dart between them and silence her brother. But she couldn't move fast enough, and Mason did what he wanted no matter who opposed him. Well, maybe not Felicity, but she hadn't come with them to move in.

"But not too close of an eye, cowboy. She's—"

"Do not finish that sentence," Charlotte said, taking angry

steps forward. She shoved against Mason's chest, and to her surprise, he fell back into the hallway. "You're done here. Go home."

"Charlotte," he chastised.

"Thank you for your help this morning," she said. "But I don't need you to unpack my clothes." She glared at Beau too, who wore an expression of mild curiosity mixed with mild horror. "I need some air."

"Char," Mason called after her as she stalked down the hall and out the back door. She burst into the morning shade at the back of the house, where the air maintained a crispness to it that would only bake away as the day wore on.

The solid cabin walls and door kept all the noise inside and the wind out, so she couldn't hear if Beau and Mason continued their conversation. She watched her step as she darted down the steps to the back yard, where Beau's two dogs lay in the shade.

The black lab got to his feet to come greet her, but his collie simply waited for Charlotte to scrub Pepper's head and jowls before she came to her. She accepted the love and greeting, but she didn't seem overly anxious to get it.

Charlotte stood in the shade and looked out over the fields. "Pretty view," she said. "Do you guys come lay here often?" The dogs didn't answer, but that didn't deter Charlotte. "Do you two know the horses? What do you think they'll think of me?"

Ruby, the collie, started to pant, and Charlotte wondered if she could leave the cabin area entirely and go meet the horses she'd be caring for.

In the end, she decided she better not. She wanted to thank all the cowboys who'd come to help her unload her car that morning, and she'd probably already been away for too long. She went back to the side of the cabin where she and Mason had parked, and she found only a few items remaining.

She'd no sooner than picked up a box marked essential oils when someone said, "Let me, ma'am."

She did let the cowboy take the box, and he gave her a smile. "I'm Bennett. Beau's best friend here on the ranch."

"Great to meet you," she said. "You're the one getting married tomorrow."

"That's right." He nodded at her and turned to take the box inside. Right behind him came another cowboy, this one much younger.

"I'm Finn Ackerman," he said pleasantly. "My parents own the ranch."

Charlotte swallowed as he picked up a laundry basket with hangers and framed photographs. "Thank you for your help."

"Of course," Finn said, as if he just loved helping a total stranger move in.

As she watched, the rest of her boxes and items got picked up and taken inside, and Charlotte had nothing else to do but follow the cowboys helping her.

She'd just reached the top of the steps and started to cross the porch to the open front door when she heard Mason say, "Yeah, her heart condition."

Panic seized her pulse, and Charlotte ran to the doorway if only to use it for support. Only Beau and Mason stood in the living room, thankfully. But Beau wore the ultimate look of confusion.

"Heart condition?" he repeated.

"She didn't tell you?" Mason's features transformed with fury and disbelief. "I can't believe this." He turned toward the back door. "Where is she?"

Beau looked to the front door, and he sure didn't look happy either. Their eyes met, and Charlotte had so much to say to him.

Don't tell anyone else, please.

I was going to tell you, I swear.

Why are you so mad about this?

"She's right there," Beau said darkly. Mason turned toward her, and if Charlotte didn't want a huge scene wherein everyone in the Texas Panhandle and all of Oklahoma would find out about her very mild heart condition, she had to act.

Fast.

So she rushed into the house and said, "You guys are over-reacting." She gestured wildly down the hall, where she assumed the other cowboys who'd come to help her move had gone. "Can we not talk about this here, right now?"

She switched her glare to her brother. "And it's not your thing to talk about at all, Mason."

"You didn't tell him," he hissed.

"Just because I don't do things according to your timeline doesn't mean I wasn't going to do it." She cut a quick look at Beau. "And you know what? It's really none of your business either."

"None of my business?"

Mason glanced past her, and movement caught her attention too. The other cowboys spilled into the room, all of them chatting about something. "She's right," he said quietly. "You two can talk about this in private."

Beau got the hint, and he nodded like his neck had suddenly turned to wood. "Fine."

"Fine," Charlotte said. Then she turned to thank the men who'd helped her bring in everything she currently had to her name. She could deal with Beau and her overbearing brother later.

Much later.

* * *

Charlotte liked the way the green grass sparkled like emeralds down at the end of the white-rock lane. The gravel at her feet looked like it had just been replaced and raked out, and uncracked sidewalks led up to every log cabin where the other cowboys and cowgirls lived here at Three Rivers Ranch.

At the end of the gravel lane, the grass of the homestead took over, and someone had already set up white folding tables and chairs, and currently, several cowboys worked on fitting together poles for a tent shade that would go over them.

More than one, it turned out. Charlotte stood on the fringes of the group and activity, as Beau had said almost nothing to her since he'd learned about her heart condition from her brother. She'd thanked everyone, grabbed her water bottle from her backpack, and taken it and her purse down the hall to her bedroom.

Her new home.

She'd spent the next ninety minutes unpacking her boxes, hanging up her clothes, arranging her photos on the provided desk, and testing out the bed. When Beau had called and said, "Lunchtime," she'd opened the door and joined him in the kitchen. "You ready?"

So she'd gotten three words from him since then, and as she watched him smile and talk with someone she hadn't met yet, he reminded her of a wolf in sheep's clothing. Because she could feel his simmering anger from where she stood.

"You must be Charlotte," a dark-haired woman said.

She looked at her fully, drowning in the woman's beauty. "Yes," she managed to scrape out of her throat.

"The new Stable Manager," she said. "We're excited to have you. Pete owns Courage Reins, and you'll probably work with him a lot."

"Sure," Charlotte said. "I met Pete this morning. Is he your husband?"

"Yes, he is." She stroked her hand down the hair of a younger boy—obviously her son. "I'm Chelsea. Squire's sister. Pete's wife. This one's mom." She grinned at her son. "Come on. No one stands on the sidelines here."

Charlotte went with Chelsea and her son, and she felt and saw the eyes of everyone else on the ranch. She hated being the new person in a crowd, but she told herself she'd only be new today. Then she'd know everyone, and they'd know her, and there'd be someone else new soon enough for everyone to gawk at.

"Squire, this is—" Chelsea started to say, but Beau practically jumped to her side.

"Charlotte," he called over her. "Our new Stable Manager." He threw a glance at Squire. "Charlotte, this is the owner of the ranch, Squire Ackerman. He's also the veterinarian here." He nodded to the woman standing next to him. "His wife, Kelly. She made your curtains and picked out your bedding."

"Thank you," Charlotte said. "It's all amazing."

"My mother made the curtains, to be fair," Kelly said with a smile. Her dirty blonde hair had been pulled up and out of the way, and her blue eyes had the sharpness of a bird of prey. She smiled, though, so she didn't seem as predatory. In fact, she seemed kind and accepting. "Welcome to Three Rivers, Charlotte. You've met Chelsea."

"And her husband Pete," Charlotte said. "He owns Courage Reins." She flashed a smile over to the brunette.

"And I met your son this morning," Charlotte said. "Finn."

Kelly practically glowed at the mention of her son, and she nodded. "Yes, he's great. Goes to Baylor, and he's just here for the summer." She glanced around. "I'm not sure where he is right now."

"Edith came out to the ranch," Squire said, but Charlotte didn't know who Edith was.

"There are a lot of us here," Beau said, gently putting his hand on her lower back. Her skin fizzed beneath her tee, and she looked at him. His perfectly trimmed beard. The perched just-so cowboy hat. The dazzling glimmer in his eye. "Come meet a couple of my good friends."

"Okay," she said.

"We're eating in five," Kelly said.

"Got it," Beau said. "Ben." He joined the group of cowboys only a few feet away. They opened up for her and Beau, and he hugged his best friend quickly. "Ben and Ellie are getting married tomorrow."

He indicated the strawberry blonde next to Ben. "An afternoon wedding, right here on the ranch, since they both work here."

"We met back at the cabin," Ben said.

"Great to meet you," Ellie said.

"Will you guys live out here once you're married?" she asked, scanning the other men in the group.

"No," Ben said, exchanging a glance with Beau. "Ellie's got a house in town, and I'm moving in with her."

"This is Stu," Beau said. "He does a lot of herd work. Next to him is Douglas. He works on the agriculture crew."

"Great to meet you," she said, shaking their hands. It seemed every cowboy had the same hat, wore a beard, some form of plaid, and blue jeans.

"Time to eat," Kelly called. "Squire, call 'em in."

"Beau?"

Charlotte's attention bounced from Kelly, to Squire, to Beau, who let loose a shrill, shockingly loud whistle. She automatically shied away from it, her pulse shooting up and then falling too fast.

She could *feel* herself crashing, and she immediately grabbed onto Beau's arm just in case she passed out. She breathed in deeply, then pushed the air out. Another breath, and while her vision fuzzed a little bit, Charlotte didn't think she'd pass out.

Around her, people moved closer and chatter slowed and stopped. She focused on the very solid muscles in Beau's arm, the only anchor she had right now. He turned into her, his body heat sinking into hers in a very comforting and enjoyable way.

His hand slid along her waist, and his voice hummed through her whole body as he asked, "Are you okay?"

She nodded, and thankfully, her legs managed to turn her body out of his embrace before too much longer. They stood right close to Squire and Kelly, which meant everyone was looking almost straight at her and Beau too.

"Welcome to lunch," Squire said. "There's no real reason today, other than we all have to eat lunch every day, so I'm just gonna have...." He glanced around and seized onto someone. "My daughter, Libby, say the prayer."

Charlotte folded her arms and ducked her head, finally feeling the weight of moving morning drift away from her. She let herself shrink until she was very small on this very large ranch, in the small town of Three Rivers, which felt absolutely huge compared to her.

Everything expanded out and out, and Charlotte let herself feel the familial vibes that existed here—and she knew.

God had led her here, to this ranch, at this time.

She belonged here. So she wasn't going to let anything—not her heart condition, not the hard conversations she might have to have because of it, nothing—stop her from being on this ranch, doing this job.

Not even the handsome cowboy beside her.

Chapter Seven

Beau's stomach felt like it might burst by the time he jogged up the steps to his front porch and went inside the cabin. Charlotte followed him, and as she closed the door, Beau sighed.

"Busy day," she said.

"Yeah," he responded. He still had plenty to attend to on the ranch, though he didn't do a ton of the feeding and care of animals, which was a twenty-four-seven job. "And we're not done."

He went around the island in the kitchen and faced her, letting all the repressed irritation and yes, downright anger, to rise through him again. "So you can't scamper down the hall and close your door until we talk about your health problems."

"First." She came to a complete stop and cocked one hip. "Don't call it a health *problem*. It's not a *problem*."

"You have a heart condition that makes you faint periodically," he shot at her. "That is so a problem, Charlotte." He planted both palms on the counter and leaned into them. "You weren't hungry the day you came to interview. You fainted because your pulse and oxygen levels dropped."

"You startled me," she said.

"So that's when it happens?"

"It...can happen for a variety of reasons," she admitted, and Beau figured they were going somewhere now. He took the glaring down a notch and unlocked his shoulders. No need to make himself look bigger if he wanted her to talk.

"It's a *very* mild heart condition," she said.

"What's the name of it?" He pulled out his phone and quickly tapped to get over to his notes.

"Are you going to write it down?"

"Yes, I am." He was not going to back down on this either. Beau looked up when she remained silent. Oh, this woman was as headstrong as she was beautiful. That only made her more attractive to him, and he lowered his phone, trying to connect some dots.

"Charlotte," he said softly. Maybe it was a growl. He wasn't exactly sure. "I am the foreman of this ranch, and everyone here is my responsibility. The thousands of cattle are my responsibility. All those horses you're going to care for are my responsibility. I get to know everything. That's just how it is." He set his phone down on the counter to hopefully put her more at ease.

"I don't want everyone to know," she said.

Beau didn't fire right back at her. "Okay," he said, wishing his mind worked faster. "Some people are going to have to know."

"Who?"

"Squire," he said instantly. "Pete. And another cowboy who spends a lot of time in the stables. Kenny. I'd tell those three up-front. Just to make sure you've got help if you need it without lengthy explanations."

"Three people."

"There might be others," he said. "Who work with the horses a lot. I can see that not everyone needs to know, and that's fine."

She regarded him, some of the fire in her stunning aquamarine eyes burning out. "Three people is fine. I just—Beau, I don't want anyone, including you, to treat me differently. I can do this job."

"I know you can," he said quickly. Her desperation for the job was abundantly clear, and Beau realized as he watched it roll across her face like a Texas thunderstorm that she really needed to prove it to him.

To herself, most likely. To Mason. To everyone.

"When people find out about my heart, they treat me differently." She reached up and brushed at her eyes in an unexpected show of emotion. "I hate it. That's why I didn't tell you."

He nodded, his compassion rearing up. "What—How do they treat you?"

Charlotte lifted her chin in a somewhat defiant move. She'd softened a little, though, and Beau could see her bluster was mostly a façade. She wanted to be treated fairly, and she wanted to show the world that she could do more than live with her brother and take care of his kids.

The whole picture appeared before Beau, and he suddenly wanted those things for her too.

"They treat me like I'm broken," she said. "I'm not broken. I don't have a problem."

She kind of did, but he wasn't going to push semantics. "Okay," he said. "But we need to work out a system or some signals or Mason said something about safe words, so that when you're in trouble and you can feel it, I can help you."

Her shoulders lifted as she took in a big lungful of air. "It's called vasovagal syncope." Everything about her sagged, and she looked over to the grandfather clock. She moved in that direction. "It's not heart disease. It's just a condition that makes my heart...freak out when I get stressed, hurt, or sometimes when I'm standing for too long."

Beau moved slowly closer to her. "Standing for too long, Charlotte?"

"I know how to pace myself, Beau." She murmured his name in a soft, pretty voice, and he wanted only for her to do it again.

He positioned himself next to her. "Low blood pressure?"

"I faint when my heart rate and-or oxygen levels and-or blood pressure drop suddenly, usually in response to something startling or surprising or stressful."

"So me walking in on you looking at these photos...." He let the words sit there, and he figured he had plenty of time and air conditioning to give Charlotte the space she needed to talk.

After a couple of minutes of the two of them standing side-by-side, she said, "I used to train and show horses, and I loved it with everything inside me."

He moved his hand slightly, and it touched hers. He audibly pulled in a breath, and then he decided to simply go for it. If she didn't want to hold his hand, she'd let him know. But Charlotte didn't pull away. She didn't move her hand back. She easily slid her palm against his, and he threaded his fingers between hers.

"I miss them so much," she said. "My parents made me quit when I passed out in the saddle during one of my competitions. From that moment on, I've been watched. I had a number of tests until the doctors figured out the heart thing."

She exhaled heavily, and Beau just wanted to wrap her up in a warm blanket and make all the ragged pieces of her smooth. "My mom limited my college classes. Then Mason and Felicity started having kids, and I went to help them."

"You have a degree," he whispered, almost like he was trying to get an injured bird to come closer.

"It took me thirteen years to get," she said. "I took classes on and off while helping with the kids. I just graduated a couple of months ago."

"That's great, sweetheart." And he meant it. He looked over to her. "That's *so* great, Charlotte."

She gave him a soft smile then, her eyes not moving from the pictures of Dolly on his credenza. "I can admit I was pretty proud of myself."

Beau returned his attention to the pictures too. "Ranch management, if my memory from your résumé serves."

"Yeah," she said. "But I just want to be with horses. I just want to train them, and feed them, and ride them." She leaned her head against his bicep, something about this so meaningful to Beau. "Thank you so much for giving me this job, Beau. I promise you I'm not going to let you down."

"Mm." He let the moment splinter, and he stepped away, dropping her hand in the process. Scratching on the back door reminded him he hadn't let the dogs in yet. "We need a system or a sign. Safe words." He went around the table and opened the back door for his hounds.

Pepper and Ruby came roaring inside like they'd been stuck outside in a tornado, and they both bent over the water bowl simultaneously to get a drink. Beau grinned at them, and then turned back to Charlotte. "Well?"

She sighed like he was being insufferable, but Beau wasn't going to budge on this. "If I'm within earshot, I'll just tell you. Or like today, I just grabbed onto you."

"Why was that?"

"The whistle," she said.

"Freaked you out."

"Freaked me out," she confirmed. "And I was just staring at those photos a few days ago, remembering so much, and Ruby touched me. That freaked me out, and I don't know. Maybe my knees were locked, and I just passed out. You should know I haven't fainted in at least six months."

"Okay," Beau said. "What if I'm not in earshot and you're struggling?"

"I'll do a hand signal," she said. "I used to do that with Mason and Felicity, if I needed help with the kids."

"All right," he said. "What kind of hand signal?"

Charlotte looked like she might lunge at him and claw his eyes out, but she didn't move. "I don't know, Beau."

His irritation kicked at him too. "My sister—not the horse-riding one—did a little ASL in school. I used to practice the letters with her. I know H is like this." He held up his hand with his first two fingers stuck together like the pillars on the capital H. "Maybe just that and lift it up? I'll know you need something."

"Fine."

He demonstrated the movement, and she nodded. He noted she didn't make the gesture, and part of him wanted to see her do it before he let her go. Another part of him yelled that he wasn't her daddy, and to let this go for now. Charlotte had some big barriers up between herself and the world. Real shields he'd have to figure out a way through.

She protected herself through anger and glaring, and Beau grinned at her. "All right," he said. "Do you want to go out to the stables?"

Everything inside her relaxed. "I thought you'd never ask."

He had several other things he wanted to ask her, but he filed the questions away—especially the personal ones—and looked at the dogs. "Come on, guys," he said to them. "Let's go show Charlotte our favorite equines."

"Oh, you can't have favorites with horses," Charlotte said, and Beau had to look at her to see if her expression matched her very serious tone. It did. In fact, she shook her head like he'd just committed the worst crime possible.

"They know it, and they will punish you for it." She nodded, her words fact, and headed for the door first. "Now, watch and learn how to get them all on your side the very first time they meet you." She gave him a grin he could only classify as flirty and headed for the front door.

Beau took a moment to watch her walk away from him, and then he moved far too fast for a man his age in his eagerness to follow her, be at her side, maybe hold her hand again.

Everything between them felt new and shiny, and he reminded himself that they *lived together* as he joined her on the porch. He couldn't move too fast or come on too strong, not if he wanted his little bird to stay close, maybe crawl into the palm of his hand, and stay awhile.

Beau had never been a super patient man, but perhaps age had helped him in that regard. Because he didn't feel a great desperate urge to ask her out, hold her hand, and see if she felt the same spark between them.

He could bide his time; she lived right across the hall, after all. And he'd rushed into things before, and he didn't need to do that here. He wouldn't.

Maybe I've learned something, Lord, he thought as Charlotte waited for him at the bottom of the steps.

"Wait," she said. "I didn't get my clipboard." She started up the steps again.

"We can just meet them," he said. "You can do a formal assessment on Monday."

She paused and looked back at him. He could tell she didn't want to do that, but she did slowly return to his side. "Okay," she said slowly.

"What are you doing tomorrow?" he asked.

"Tomorrow? I don't know."

"Do you want to go to Ben's wedding with me?" Beau used everything he had to stop himself from clearing his throat. He couldn't believe he'd asked her out, when he'd literally just told himself not to.

But he didn't need to clarify. Or hem and haw and make excuses. Or ask anything again.

He just needed to wait.

Chapter Eight

Charlotte held up the phone so Felicity could see her reflection in the mirror. "Well?"

"That's a great color on you, Char," her sister-in-law said. "Purple suits you."

"It's the only thing I have, and it's from your wedding." The dress she'd pulled from an unpacked garment bag at the back of her closet had weathered the years really well. Probably because she hadn't worn it again since the day her brother got married.

"No wonder I love it," Felicity said, and Charlotte caught the tail end of her smile. "Seriously, Char, you look amazing. I can't believe you can still fit into that."

"I was bloated from all the meds they had me on when you and Mace got married," she said. "I think I weigh less now."

"How are you doing?" Felicity asked, and somehow, when she asked, Charlotte's hackles didn't get raised. But if she had been her momma, or Mason, or even worse, Beau, Charlotte would've come up with both fists swinging.

"Good," she said. "I mean, I've been here one day. But good. I got to meet all the horses yesterday. They all love me, of course."

"Of course," Felicity said with a giggle. "You took them strawberry candies."

Charlotte didn't deny it. "I know I can be good at this job."

"I know that too, sweetie." Felicity sighed and added, "Okay, I have to jet. The timer on the oven is going off. We wish you were here for dinner."

"I wish I was too." Charlotte sank onto her bed, which she'd slept on great last night. "But Felicity, I really like it here so far."

"I'm so glad." She gave her a warm smile, and they waved at one another until Felicity ended the video call.

Charlotte took a moment to just sit and let things sink in, and then she got to her feet so she could finish her makeup and put on her earrings. Bennett and Ellie were getting married right here at Three Rivers Ranch, and Beau said he'd knock on her door and "pick her up" for the wedding at four o'clock.

"Is this a date?" she wondered aloud as she brushed foundation the same color as her skin across her cheeks and chin. He'd asked her to the wedding. He'd held her hand. He looked at her with the male edge of desire she hadn't seen in a while but certainly recognized.

She'd just stepped into her shoes—a pair of clear heels that didn't really match the dress. She didn't have anything else, though, not for a wedding she'd been asked to attend yesterday —when a knock sounded on her door.

Charlotte hadn't lived alone for a great many years, so knocking on her door didn't startle her that much. Her pulse did speed a bit now, because never had she had the hottest cowboy in the state standing on the other side of that door. Usually it was a child who needed something, or her brother wanting to talk to her for a quick minute.

Now, she moved to the door and opened it, holding onto the side of it so she could lean her hip into it. She cocked her knee and stood on one toe as she smiled at Beau. "Hey, handsome."

"Hey," fell from his lips. He stared at her and then let his gaze slide down the dress to the clear shoes. "Aren't you a pretty bird?"

She laughed lightly and hung her head. "It is a wedding, cowboy."

"Sure is." He offered her his arm, his smile already faltering. "I can't be late. He's my best friend, and I'm the best man."

"I love the bowtie."

"Thanks," Beau said dryly.

"You didn't have to take the rest of them down, you know." Charlotte looked at the blank space on the wall in the hall where they'd been.

"I think I was ready for it," he said.

"What were they?"

"Bowties from all the weddings I've been to," he said. "From other cowboys here on the ranch. Some guys are still here; some have moved on."

Charlotte heard the nostalgia in his voice, and she realized that Beau viewed his ranch friends, his cowboys, the way she viewed Felicity, Mason, and the kids—as family. "How long have you been here?" she asked.

"In Texas, about twenty-three years," he said. "At Three Rivers, let's see...coming up on nineteen years." He walked slowly down the steps to give her time to place her foot just right in the heels. The gravel wasn't going to be fun either, and Charlotte regretted her footwear choice.

"Do you remember meeting me?" she asked, her voice hardly sounding like her own. "I came to town with Mason a few times. You...." She trailed off, because she didn't like where she'd been headed.

"I remember," he said. "Vaguely." They moved slowly down the gravel lane, and already Charlotte could hear twinkling music. The ranch held a vibrancy and life that only a wedding could bring, and she took in all the sights and sounds at the same time.

The bright blue sky, the striking green grass ahead, the classic red barn on the end. Beyond that, she could hear the music, and the sound of cars and trucks arriving, and if she listened hard, the din of voices who'd already gathered and were mingling.

"You must like it here," she said when he didn't go on about their first meeting when she was fifteen years old.

"I love it here," he said. "I mean, anywhere is better than a ranch in New Mexico, so." He chuckled. "But Three Rivers is my home now. The ranch, the town. I love it."

They arrived on the lawn, and Charlotte was glad to stand

for a moment to take in the scene. Balloons and streamers waved in the wind, but she didn't see any tents, tables, or chairs. "Where are they getting married?"

Beau nodded over to the huge riding and training facility across the street—Courage Reins. "The big barn over there."

She detected something in his voice, but when she looked at him, he wore nothing but the pure shininess of a newly minted copper penny. "Will there be dancing?" she asked.

Beau looked at her then, his thoughts coming closer to the present than they'd been a moment ago. She could just see it in his eyes. "Sure will."

"Are you a good dancer, Mister Peterson?"

"Yes, ma'am," he said with a smile. He started moving toward the edge of the lawn that met the dirt road, and she went easily with him.

"And modest about it too."

"My momma said it was okay to admit when you're good at something," he said. "Doesn't mean I'm bragging. I'm just saying I'm good at it."

"So...will you dance with me at the wedding tonight?"

"Depends," he said.

"On what?"

"If it's going to freak out your heart."

Charlotte wanted to snap back at him, but then he added, "Because my pulse is already goin' nuts with you on my arm, so maybe we should do a raincheck."

She dang near fell down, and she looked at him with wide eyes. "Your...what?"

"Let's talk about it after," he murmured just before he

went into full public-relations mode and said hello to Ethan Greene and his wife, Brynn. They had three children with them, all pre-teens if Charlotte could predict ages. Since she'd been nannying kids that same age for a while, she felt certain she could.

The real Beau Peterson disappeared behind the foreman version of him, and Charlotte mourned his loss. Still, he was handsome and funny, charismatic and outgoing, and she enjoyed being next to him as they mingled with others from the ranch.

Everyone flicked their eyes to her for a moment, but no one made any comments about her being there with him, and she'd moved her hand out of his arm before they'd reached the grass. She thought about his racing pulse, the look he slid her every so often, and the way he'd invited her to this wedding.

If they weren't dating yet, he definitely wanted to start. And Charlotte found she wanted that too. She hadn't been out with anyone in a long time—nannying four children and living with her brother wasn't a great breeding ground for romance.

She barely knew which way was up right now, and she told herself she had plenty of time. So she could enjoy this wedding, start her new job, and figure out how to live with the cowboy for more than twenty-four hours before she started a romantic relationship with him.

"I have to go line up," he said, leaning his head down and creating an intimate bubble between them. "I'll be back in a bit. Save me a chair?"

"Up front?"

"The wedding party is up front, yes." He raised his head

then, and Charlotte caught a flicker of unrest in those beautiful eyes. Beau walked away without saying anything else, leaving Charlotte to find her way to the rows of chairs with the altar up front.

Not that it was hard. The crowd swept her along, each cowboy and his lady wearing something fancy and fine. Their Sunday-best hats, and more black suit jackets than Charlotte had seen even at church.

She found a few rows up front that only held women, and she suspected their cowboys would make up the wedding party. She walked on her glass heels and approached, leaning down to say to one woman, "If my...the man I'm with is in the wedding party, can I sit here?"

"Sure thing," she said with a smile. She indicated the rest of her row, which was third from the front. "I need to be on the end for my husband."

"No problem," Charlotte said as she squeezed by her. "I don't know—we'll be fine wherever." She figured Beau would have to walk around and over people all day, so it didn't really matter. Everyone would be doing it once they came in.

"Who are you here with?" the woman asked. "I need three seats. My sons are in the line too."

Charlotte moved down another chair and set her phone on the one she needed for Beau. "Uh, I came with my cabinmate, Beau Peterson."

"Oh, you must be Charlotte." The woman's whole face brightened, and she leaned over the trio of empty chairs between them. "I'm Juliette Ahlstrom. Garth's wife."

Charlotte simply smiled and shook her hand. "Nice to meet you."

"Garth and I used to live in your cabin," she said. "He was the foreman here before Beau."

Dots lined up to create a picture, and Charlotte's smile widened. "Oh, of course. I literally moved in yesterday. I don't know anything about anything yet."

"You will," Juliette promised. "Soon enough." She sat up straight in her seat and slid her hand down the silver fabric of the dress she wore. "You got moved in okay?"

"Yes, ma'am."

"And how's Beau doing?"

Charlotte opened her mouth to answer, then found she didn't have one. "I...don't know. How should he be?"

"He and Ben have been best friends for years," Juliette said as she peered behind her to see if the wedding procession was about to start. "They've lived together forever, right up until Beau moved into the foreman's cabin. I'd expect him to be moody."

"Moody?"

Juliette looked at her, and Charlotte honestly didn't know what else to say. "Yes," Juliette said. "You know how cowboys are when their worlds get shaken up. They go silent. Then they get mad over silly things." She smiled and giggled and shook her head. "My boys do the same thing, though I keep telling them there are other ways to work through your emotions."

Charlotte smiled too. She nodded too. "Oh, I get it. Sure, of course." But she hadn't seen Beau acting "moody."

Of course, she hardly knew Beau Peterson, so she certainly wasn't the best judge of his behavior. Thankfully, the wedding started, and she got to her feet to see Bennett leading the way down the aisle.

A bit odd, slightly off-script, but he wore a smile the size of the great state of Texas, and he led only cowboys. No women. No pairs. Just Bennett surrounded by cowboys.

Beau was second in line, and that told Charlotte where he ranked in his best friend's life too. Mason had talked about Beau plenty, as they'd stayed friends since their days together in college. But seeing him with Bennett was a whole new ball game. He clearly loved his friend, and when they reached the altar, Beau grabbed onto Bennett and hugged him hard.

No one tried to get him to step back. He faced Charlotte, and she watched his mouth move as he whispered something to Bennett. The other cowboy nodded and hugged Beau back just as hard.

And she knew then that while this wedding was an amazing thing, a beautiful union of two people who loved each other deeply, it also cut like a hot knife. This was something separating Beau from someone he loved, and while they both knew it would be okay, it wasn't right now.

She couldn't look away from him as Beau finally let go and shuffled out of the way so the other men could congratulate Ben. Only a minute later, the men started making their way onto the first three rows, and Beau spotted her, fixed his bowtie —the eighteenth one he'd worn for a wedding here at the ranch —and made his way toward her past Garth and his teenagers.

Charlotte didn't know what to say to make things better.

Sometimes words simply didn't do a good enough job. So she linked her arm through his and stayed standing while the most gorgeous bride in the world strolled down the aisle to her forever cowboy.

As she sat and Beau slid his hand into hers, Charlotte acknowledged that part of her getting a new job and moving out on her own included finding someone to love the way Ellie obviously loved Bennett.

She forced herself not to look at Beau, but she couldn't stop her mind from spinning questions like, *What if it's Beau Peterson? What if he could be your knight in shining armor? Your Prince Charming? The cowboy who sees you, accepts you, and loves you no matter how many times you faint or how stubborn you are about training horses?*

What if it's him and you've already met him? What if? What if? What if?

Chapter Nine

Beau kept his eyes wide open as he danced with Charlotte. Ben's wedding had been perfect from beginning to end, and he was glad for his friend. Truly. He wanted to sink into the apple blossom scent of Charlotte's hair and drift lazily back to their cabin together, but he had a bigger, more knowing audience than would allow him to act like he had in his younger years.

He didn't want to be that twenty-something anyway.

"Are you ready to go?" he asked as the last notes of the song faded.

"Are you?"

"Yes," he said honestly. "We've been here long enough. Ben won't care." He turned to find his friends, and thankfully, they were only a few paces away. He went toward them and wrapped both Ben and Ellie into the same hug. "Love you guys. We'll see you when you get back from New Orleans."

They weren't going far, nor for long, as neither of them had much money. But Beau couldn't remember a day out of the last eighteen years that he hadn't seen and talked to Bennett. Tomorrow would be the first one.

His emotions clapped like angry thunder, and Beau couldn't wait to leave the public eye. He just wanted a silent cabin without lights on and a really good hamburger.

"Love you, Beau," both Ben and Ellie said, and then he faced Charlotte again. She said her more formal good-byes, and they left the party. He took her the back way in front of the barns and stables to their cabin, and he said nothing along the way.

He loosened his bowtie the moment he got behind a wall separating him from everyone else on the ranch, and he had it off and his shirt unbuttoned by the time he reached the steps. At the porch, his jacket was coming off, and the moment he stepped inside, he felt like he could breathe again.

He walked toward the hall, semi-forgetting he wasn't alone until the door closed behind him. "Oh." He turned back to Charlotte, his shirt untucked and undone and his hands full of his jacket and tie. "I'm going to go shower."

"Okay," she said.

He wasn't used to giving an accounting of what he was doing and why, so he left her there. "What's she going to do?" he wondered. Of course she'd have to change out of that pretty party dress. Take off her makeup, maybe. Beau didn't rightly know what women did to "dress down" and get more comfortable.

They'd spent last night eating dinner and watching TV, and he figured they could do the same tonight.

When he returned to the kitchen, the scent of coffee beckoned to him, and he wore a pair of gym shorts and a gray t-shirt with the Three Rivers logo on it. He didn't see Charlotte anywhere, but he figured he could pour himself a cup of coffee in his own cabin.

He'd no sooner done that before his phone chimed. He picked it up and saw Charlotte had texted. *I made coffee, so help yourself.*

Do you want to be alone tonight? I'm fine to stay in my room to give you your space.

He looked up from the texts to find his dogs both sitting beside their food bowl. He was late feeding them, so he flew into motion to do that. Did he want to be alone tonight?

Beau honestly wasn't sure. He didn't want Charlotte to feel like she had to sequester herself in her bedroom, but he was used to having free rein of everything in the house.

After feeding his hounds, he typed out a message to Charlotte. *You can do what you want. I'm fine. We'll go help the vacation crew feed the horses in about an hour. Or I will. You don't have to do anything until tomorrow.*

Her official start date.

She didn't answer, and Beau turned to the fridge, though he'd eaten a full meal only an hour ago at the wedding.

"I'll come," Charlotte said from behind him, and he nudged the fridge closed as he turned to face her. She wore a pair of jean shorts that went all the way to her knee and a tank top the color of the apple-y scent she put off. Bright red.

"You don't have to hide in your room," he said. "Ever. This is your house too."

"I thought you might want your space."

"If I don't want to be around anyone, *I* can go to *my* room."

"Fair enough." She moved to the other side of the counter. "Is it hard? Having him get married?"

Beau blinked, the question out of left field for him. No one had ever asked it outright like that. "Yes," he said just as bluntly. "He's been my roommate and best friend for a long time."

She nodded, her expression unreadable. "Are you dating anyone right now?"

His eyes widened now, and he leaned back against the fridge. "Am I dating anyone right now? Do you think I'd hold your hand if I was?"

"I don't know."

Irritation foamed through him. "Okay, well, I wouldn't. Who would do that to someone—both the person they were dating and the person they weren't? Or wanted to? Or...I don't know. It's a weird question."

Charlotte finally dropped her gaze, her cheeks turning bright red in the next moment. "You're right. It was a weird question. I haven't been out much lately."

"Out much? Like in public or with a man?"

"Both." She turned away from him. "I'm going for a walk." She wore the sneakers to do it too, and Beau simply watched her go.

"Okay," he said when she opened the door. She didn't say she'd see him later, and he honestly wasn't sure what had just happened. Once the door sealed him back in his cabin alone, breathing did feel easier. "Maybe she's just a little awkward," he told himself.

But she hadn't been awkward in that dress or heels. She knew how to greet strangers and ask them about themselves. She'd been a full participant in the wedding, the conversation at dinner, and all through the dancing.

"So maybe she's exhausted too," he said. And maybe she hadn't been out with anyone in a while. He'd learned to gather as much intel as possible over the years, but there was no way he was going to text Mason and ask him about his sister's dating history.

Absolutely no way. Mason had already made it quite clear that he didn't want Beau to take his relationship with Charlotte past professional, and his fingers tingled where she'd touched them.

"You're both adults," he told himself as he sat on the couch and held his phone in front of him. He had other people to text, and he busied himself with that until it was time to go feed the horses. Charlotte didn't show up, and Beau let himself turn into the fanciful dreamer he'd always been.

And he saw the two of them horseback riding, running and laughing through fields, before they came back to this cabin together and he kissed her good-night.

Definitely a dream, and a good one. *Maybe one that could come true*, he thought. *Yeah...maybe.*

"There he is," Preacher Glover said when he opened the door to his beautiful, new farmhouse. "Howdy, Beau." He grinned in a rare display and stepped out onto the porch to give Beau a hug.

"Howdy, Preach." He clapped the man on the back softly, so as to not make his bad leg buckle. "Something smells amazing inside."

"Holly Ann catered dinner for us."

"You're joking." Beau stepped back. "I'd have been here an hour ago if I'd have known."

"She just brought it," Ace said. He'd married Holly Ann several years ago, and they had two kids now. In fact, she was pregnant with their third and would have the baby this fall.

Beau stepped into the house and hugged Ace too. "Thanks for getting us dinner."

"Holly Ann's already filling every fridge and freezer up here at Shiloh Ridge." Ace grinned and indicated his wife standing at the back wall, in front of the kitchen sink. Charlie, Preacher's wife lingered there with her, their two-year-old clinging to her pant leg as if Hank never saw strangers.

And Beau wasn't a stranger here. Hank loved him; he simply looked like he'd been crying.

She and Preacher had just announced they'd welcome another baby to their family this winter, and Beau had congratulated them heartily via text.

Beau had gotten used to literally everyone around him getting married and building families—he'd literally been a witness to it for almost two decades now—and it had never bothered him.

Until the past several years, that was. Until he'd finally matured enough to want those things for himself.

Charlie caught sight of him, and she came into the living room. She grinned from ear to ear, Hank stumbling after her. "Did you get into the inner sanctum?"

"Twice," Beau said as he smiled back. He bent down and swooped Hank into his arms. "Heya, buddy."

The little boy smiled, and sure enough, Beau's heart pinched with want. Then it howled. He couldn't even imagine how he'd feel if he held his own child, but it was something he wanted to experience badly.

"How was the wedding?" Preacher asked. He had a way of driving nails straight into the heart, because as one of the foremen at Shiloh Ridge, he didn't believe in beating around any bushes.

"Fine," Beau said as he lifted his eyes to Preacher's. "Good, even."

"How are you?" Preach asked next.

"I'm...coping," Beau admitted. Ben had been out of town for a week, but he'd been at work today. Beau had eaten lunch with him even. Heard all about New Orleans and the big river boats.

"Did you get a Stable Manager?"

"Is this going to be the extent of the questioning?" Beau gave him a dry look and then switched his gaze to Charlie. "If I answer everything now, can we eat and play without the interrogation?"

Her grin didn't so much as falter. "I'm sure that's Preacher's plan."

Preacher didn't apologize, and he didn't back down. He simply stood back a few feet, and when little Hank reached for him saying, "Daddy, see Rex," he switched his attention to him. He didn't take him from Beau, probably because his back couldn't handle lifting someone or something as big as a two-year-old.

"No, son," he said. "Rex is asleep for the night."

"Like you will be soon," Charlie said, reaching to take Hank into her arms. "Let's eat." She threw Beau a look that said she knew he had more questions to answer, and he wasn't sure if he wanted to stay, but outside Ben and Garth—neither of whom lived at Three Rivers Ranch anymore—these were his best friends.

He'd been playing online games with them for years, and he even tried a brief relationship with Ace's sister, Etta. That had been a disaster, and Beau hadn't tried to meet anyone new since then.

He hadn't tried to meet Charlotte either, and as they shifted toward the dining room table, he said, "I met someone."

Preacher stilled, only his eyes drifting up to meet Beau's. "Oh?"

"Is everyone going to want to hear the story?"

"I'm sure," Preacher said. "You've met my family, right?" He rolled his eyes and led the way toward the table. "Charlie, Beau's met someone new."

As if Preacher didn't love the drama and gossip as much as everyone else. Beau chuckled and shook his head as he joined everyone at the dining room table. "It so happens that she's my new Stable Manager." He pulled out a chair beside Ace and sat down. "And she, uh, *we* didn't have anywhere for her to stay, so she's living with me."

Beau picked up his napkin and snapped it open, aware of the complete silence around him. No one even moved, and only Ace had sat down. He laid his napkin in his lap and looked up to find Holly Ann frozen only a couple of feet from the table, a large bowl of salad in her hands.

Charlie had been buckling Hank into his booster seat, and Preacher had his hand on the back of his chair, as if he'd pull it out at any moment. But none of them moved. Or spoke.

Betty, the five-year-old, didn't get the memo, and she loudly scraped her chair over the tile as she pulled it out and started to climb up to the table.

Beau chuckled, glad he'd caused such a reaction. "What are y'all most surprised about? That I met someone new? That I got a great Stable Manager? Or that we're sharing a cabin?"

Only a beat of time passed before Preacher said, "I'm only surprised about the cabin thing."

"Three bedrooms, two baths," he said. "It's not scandalous or anything." Words he'd said to his mother too. She'd had a lot more questions for Beau, and to be fair, he hadn't told her he had sparking feelings for Charlotte. He wasn't going to use those words tonight either, and thankfully, Holly Ann put the salad on the table.

"I think it's great you met someone," she said as she took her seat on the other side of Ace. "Now, tonight, Ace said he needed brain food to get through the inner sanctum, so I've made a kale, apple, and cranberry salad as a starter."

Preacher and Charlie sat down too, both of them looking at him. "I'll say grace," Preach said.

"And we won't ask any more questions," Charlie promised.

"Tonight," Preacher said. He cocked one eyebrow at Beau, who only grinned back at him. Then he bowed his head for grace, the start of a hopefully great evening of food, friends, and games ahead of him.

As the night unfolded into exactly that, Beau found that he couldn't wait to get back to the cabin and tell Charlotte about his friends. As he made the turn after the ninety-minute drive back to the ranch, he wondered, "Maybe she could come with me next time."

He didn't go to Shiloh Ridge often, because it was a long drive, and he was a busy man. They played online, which he could do from the comfort of his own cabin, any time of day or night.

But maybe next time, when he did go to Preacher's or Ace's for dinner and gaming, Charlotte could come with him.

"You better tell her about your live-streaming and your gaming then," he told himself. He'd lost girlfriends over his video games in the past, so it could be an issue for her. Of course, he hadn't asked her out yet either. They simply spent time together in the place where they both lived, and he'd been getting to know her.

Perhaps it was time for things to change, and Beau searched for his next move to get the future he wanted.

Chapter Ten

Charlotte woke early in the morning, the way she always did. No matter how early she got up, Beau's bedroom door stood open. This morning was no exception, and she glanced across the hall and then went into the bathroom.

She didn't know where he went in the morning, but she'd never found him in the kitchen. His dogs were never there either, and she hadn't found a spare moment to ask him. She'd been at Three Rivers now for two weeks, and there always seemed to be fifteen hundred things happening on this ranch.

When she'd asked Beau about that, he'd chuckled and said, "Yeah, about." They weren't the biggest ranch in the Panhandle, but coming in second meant they were quite huge indeed. Charlotte had over forty horses to care for, and she'd gone through the notebooks and files for each of them, then started adding to them.

She felt it important to build a rapport with each and every equine, and that took copious amounts of time. She had to learn their personalities; they had to learn hers. They had to learn to trust her; she had to learn to trust them.

With so many horses, she couldn't spend significant time with each of them every day, so she'd put them on a schedule where she got at least a half-hour with every horse every third day. Some of them obeyed instantly, but some had a stubborn streak that would take a bit more time for her to overcome.

They were working horses for sure, and that meant any cowboy or cowgirl should be able to swing into the saddle and get the job done.

Charlotte finished brushing her teeth, and she returned to her room to get dressed. Sure enough, the kitchen held a half-pot of coffee, and she poured herself a cup and added cream and sugar as she looked out the window above the sink. Movement caught her attention in the pre-dawn light, and she thought it was Ruby's bushy collie tail.

It could also be a fox or a coyote, but they didn't usually venture so close to humans—and out of cover, where they could hide. Feeling adventurous—and she'd get to see the sunrise this morning—Charlotte left the cabin through the back door.

Looking left, she found Ruby trotting along behind cabin row. Alone. "Odd," she said to herself. Ruby never went anywhere without Pepper, and both of them stuck to Beau like glue.

The dog went around the corner of a cabin, and Charlotte went down the steps, her curiosity off the charts. Then Pepper came tearing out of the gap, a ball flying ahead of him and bouncing in the field, where he dashed to retrieve it.

Ruby didn't reappear, and once Pepper had returned the ball, he didn't get to chase it again.

Charlotte went past cabin after cabin, realizing that Beau and his dogs had to be on the lawn of the homestead. When she finally made it past the last cabin, she found him sitting in a lawn chair at a firepit, both dogs lying beside him.

And he had a tripod set up with his phone on it, all four of them facing the rising sun. No one else seemed to be anywhere in the vicinity, and Beau lifted the lid of his thermos to his lips and took a sip.

Then his mouth moved, and surprise streamed through Charlotte. "What is he doing?"

Beau set his coffee down in the rocks, got up, and adjusted the phone. Then he picked up a red Frisbee and tossed it out in front of him, clearly in line of the phone—he was recording something—and Ruby went after it.

He wore pure happiness on his face, and again, he spoke.

Deciding to find out what was going on, Charlotte started to cross the lawn. Ruby caught the Frisbee and brought it back, and once Beau had it in his hand, he looked over to her. Surprise crossed his face, and he kept talking.

As she neared, she heard him say, "...we're only about forty-five seconds away now, folks. The sky is so pretty this morning, ain't it?"

Oh, the cowboy drawl was enunciated, and Charlotte paused on the edge of the gravel, lest her boots make too much noise on it and ruin his recording.

"We've got someone new with us this morning," he said. Charlotte noticed the scrolling comments on his phone then.

Hearts and thumbs-up emojis kept flitting onto the screen and rising like steam too.

He was broadcasting. Live-streaming. Confusion puckered her brow. For who? And what?

"And here we are, folks," he said. "Six-fifty-four a.m., the prettiest sunrise in the world, I think, what with all those stringy clouds in the low horizon. Straight to you from the Texas Panhandle."

He paused for a moment, looking at his phone and not her, and continued with, "I am at the homestead this morning. It was an excellent view of the clouds. I'll try to get out to the creek later this week."

Another pause, and then he answered another comment. After a few minutes of this, Beau said, "All right, ladies and gents. This cowboy's gotta get to work." He plucked the phone off the tripod and turned it around to face him. "And look, the new Stable Manager here at the ranch joined us. Say hi, Charlotte."

She lifted her hand, no idea if she was in the frame or not. "Hi."

Beau grinned at his phone and said, "Until tomorrow's sunrise, have a good one, doing good things and living good lives." He waited a couple of seconds as comments positively streamed up his phone. More emojis than Charlotte had ever seen in her life followed, and then Beau ended the live-stream.

Beau transformed in front of her. His shoulders relaxed and went down. He sighed and shoved his phone in his pocket. He turned to face her with a hint of resignation in his expression. "Nice sunrise today," he said.

He came to her side on the fringe of the gravel, and they both faced into it as the golden light bathed the land in front of them.

"It is," she said.

"So I live-stream the sunrise every morning," he said. "I'm the Sunrise Cowboy."

Charlotte let a puff of air out that sounded harsher than she intended. "That's—wow."

"Unexpected," he said.

"Yeah," she said. "I mean, I didn't—it's not like you don't know how to use technology."

"People tune in from all over the world," he said. "They're fascinated by the American cowboy way."

"Are they now?" She grinned into the morning light.

"Seem to be," he said. "It's about twenty minutes is all. I bring out my coffee and my dogs. Set up in a different spot most days, and we…talk."

"You have online friends," she teased.

"A lot of 'em." He chuckled. "I have in-person friends too."

"Mm." Charlotte wanted to ask if she was one of them, but she wanted to be more than friends too. "Beau?"

"Yep."

"Let's go have breakfast."

"Yes, ma'am." He gathered his tripod and his dog toys quickly, and they made the walk back to the cabin they shared. She pulled out a package of bacon and started laying strips in the hot pan while he gave his dogs fresh water and their breakfast.

She sliced tomatoes and tore lettuce, turned the bacon and

set bread in the toaster. Beau sat at the counter and typed on his phone, finally setting it aside as the first slices of toast popped up.

"BLTs?" he asked.

"Yes." She cut him a look and got the mayo out of the fridge.

"For breakfast?"

"Don't you eat sandwiches for breakfast? I swear I've seen you make sausage and egg sandwiches for breakfast. Just last week, in fact."

"Yeah, but—"

She waited, but he didn't continue. "But what? This is a bacon sandwich."

"No eggs." He wore a flirty smile, and oh, Charlotte could fall into that easily.

"Do you want me to scramble you some eggs?"

"No, ma'am."

"Good." She spread mayo on the toast and plucked a handful of strips of bacon from the pan. She assembled his sandwich quickly and slid the plate toward him. She still had to make her toast, and the bacon was in very real danger of getting burnt.

She took care of that, and then set her bread to toast. Beau waited for her to finish her sandwich and sit beside her, and then he looked her straight in the eye and said, "I'd like to go out with you. What do you think of me and you goin' to dinner one day this week?"

He swallowed, and it felt like someone had turned the

lights up in the cabin. All the way to bright white. She blinked, and the cabin settled back into normal hues.

"Oh, boy." He chuckled. "Are you going to pass out? Did I startle you too much?"

She picked up the knife she'd used for the mayo and cut her sandwich in half. "A little is all."

"A little?" he teased. "Don't tell me you haven't felt this fizzing thing between us."

She looked over to him, and he sobered. "I mean that. If you haven't felt it, don't tell me. Just say no to dinner, and we'll eat, and everything will be fine."

Charlotte liked the way he drawled out *fine*, and she couldn't keep up the stoic act. She smiled too and said, "I've felt it."

Relief sagged through him. "Praise the heavens." He picked up his whole sandwich. "I'm free any night this week."

"As am I."

"Then tomorrow," he said.

"Tomorrow is fine," she said, trying to mimic his cowboy accent. She didn't quite make it, and he laughed and nudged her with his elbow.

"Don't tease me," he said.

"Oh, like you don't tease me."

"Well, I can't have you fainting when I knock on your bedroom door to take you out," he said. "Or have you going limp in my arms when I'm about to kiss you...." He raised his eyebrows, his smile glorious and filling the kitchen with light.

Charlotte's cells vibrated with desire—and a little bit of

fear. It had been so long since she'd kissed a man, and surely someone like Beau had had a lot of girlfriends.

He chuckled and said, "Okay, I won't tease you about it."

"How long have you been live-streaming?"

"Oh, gosh." He exhaled and looked up and to the right. "Three years now, I think."

"I see."

"You could come out with me if you want," he said.

Charlotte smiled at him. "I don't want to step on your feet."

"I just invited you."

"Okay," she said.

"Okay." He finished his sandwich, and then looked at her. "Tell me something I don't know about you."

"Can we trade back and forth?"

"Sure."

Which meant he had more secrets. Charlotte had plenty of her own, so she finished her bite of bacon, lettuce, and tomato, and said, "I like to sing to the horses."

Beau grinned and added, "And in the shower."

Charlotte looked at him with surprise running through her. It didn't make her heart rate crash or her blood sugar drop. "You've heard me?"

"Sweetheart, the walls aren't that thick here." He grinned at her. "You have a great voice."

"Do I?"

"Sure," he said. "If you like to sing, I know a pastor who does a big Christmas concert. She's always looking for singers."

Charlotte wanted to do that, and she said, "I could be persuaded to audition for that."

"Great," Beau said. "We can go to church on the south side of town. She preaches down there with her brother."

"I'd like that," Charlotte murmured. "Is that where you normally go to church?"

"No," he said. "But it doesn't matter. It's just more time to drive through town. I'll go anywhere you want."

"Your turn," she said. "Something I don't know about you."

"I like to play online video games," he said. "Remember I told you about going to Shiloh Ridge last week?"

"Oh, sure."

"I do it at home mostly," he said. "Keeps me busy in a different way than ranch work, and it's fun."

"Do you know everyone you play with?"

"For the most part," he said. "Yeah."

Charlotte finished her sandwich and got up to put the plates in the sink and clean up the leftover leaves of lettuce and the butt end of the tomato. "I'll eat that," he said as she picked it up.

"This?" She handed him the tomato. "Just...one bite?"

"Well, probably three." He took the first one, and Charlotte couldn't help smiling.

"Gross," she said.

"You just ate it on a sandwich."

"That's not the same as biting into a tomato like it's an apple." She turned and put the cutting board in the sink. "Where will we go to dinner tomorrow?"

"I don't know," he said. "What do you like?"

Charlotte faced him again. "You know what sounds amazing?"

"Do tell."

"A loaded baked potato," she said. "One of those big ones that they rub salt all over the peel, and that's almost as good as the buttery, creamy inside, with cheese and bacon and green onions. Oh, and ranch dressing. Lots of ranch dressing."

Beau laughed, the sound full and throaty, and Charlotte sure did like it. It seemed to fill a hole inside her she hadn't realized was quite so empty—and that only he could fill.

"I know just the place for that, little bird." He gave her a grin and then got to his feet. "I have to get over to the admin building. New assignments being made today." He went to the row of pegs running toward the kitchen from the front door, picked up a hat, and settled it on his head.

He turned back and saluted while Pepper and Ruby waited for him to open the door, everything about him magnetic and drawing her closer. "You're working that new horse this afternoon?"

"Yes."

"If I have time, I'll come over." Then he left the cabin with his dogs, and Charlotte fell back against the sink behind her. Her heart pounded, but she didn't feel faint. Everything felt more alive than it ever had, which was the opposite of how she usually felt when she was about to pass out.

A slow smile curved her mouth, and she spun to look out the window to the view she'd grown quite fond of in the past couple of weeks. "Thank you," she whispered. "For bringing me to this ranch. For making it so I could meet Beau, for the horses here."

So much gratitude and joy filled her that tears flooded Charlotte's eyes. Her future had never seemed so wide open, and she never even dreamed she'd have an experience like the past two weeks.

She'd been taught that God had a plan for her life, and He'd never lead her astray. She'd felt so caged inside her existence for the past few years, but now she wondered if the Lord had just been holding her for a bit, until both she and Beau were ready for her to arrive on this ranch.

"I believe in Thy plans," she whispered. And she did. Her faith had been restored in a loving, kind God who only wanted the best for her.

Now, she just had to figure out if Beau Peterson fit into that plan.

Chapter Eleven

Beau left the administration building and hurried down the steps. He'd just gotten a text from Finn that Charlotte had been working with one of their new horses "brilliantly" for the past several minutes.

Quite the crowd had gathered at the training ring where she had the tan-colored horse. He had darker brown hair that looked like it had been cut into shags and bangs, and Charlotte and another cowboy named Robbie both stood in the ring with the equine.

The other cowboys sat on the fence or clung to it, and Beau boosted himself up onto the rungs next to Finn.

"Hey," he said to the much younger man. He reminded Beau a little bit of himself—always with the positive outlook on life, full of laughter and smiles—and Finn turned toward him.

"Hey." He looked back into the ring. "She's so patient with them. It rivals Pete."

Beau nodded and asked, "Did you guys get the salt licks out?"

"Yep," Finn said. "Got back about twenty minutes ago."

"Great." Beau refocused his attention back in the ring where Charlotte and Robbie worked with the horse.

Valentine came to them from an overcrowded stable, and while the ranch didn't normally get unbroken horses, she'd definitely been one of the wilder ones. She could take a bit and accept riders, but she didn't like it. They'd only had her for a few days, and Charlotte had been trying to win over the equine from the first minute she'd arrived on the ranch.

Even now, she stood back and let Robbie use the flag to move the horse closer to her. Charlotte stood almost at the rail, and she looked dusty, sweaty, and downright gorgeous. Beau hadn't dated a lot of cowgirls—legit cowgirls—in his life, as he preferred a more girly, feminine woman.

Or, at least he thought he had. But watching Charlotte in her blue jeans and steel-toed work boots, her long-sleeved shirt that absolutely came from the men's section at The Boot Barn, and that oversized hat, and he dang near swooned right off the fence.

He climbed up and sat on the top rung like some of the other cowboys, content to watch for a few minutes. He couldn't believe he'd finally gotten up the nerve to lay some of his feelings out on the table, but it sure had felt good to do so. He figured now that Charlotte knew about his live-streaming, he didn't have too much more to hide.

Beau watched intently as Valentine circled around, her movements fluid but edged with a wildness that had yet to be fully tamed. The horse's mane flicked with each defiant turn, embodying the freedom she so fiercely clung to, and dust lifted into the air from her hooves. Beau's admiration for Charlotte grew with each passing second, with each time Robbie sent Valentine over to her and the equine dodged back; Charlotte's patience became a quiet force in the ring that expanded outward, her presence both calming and assertive.

Robbie looked at Charlotte, who gave him another nod, clearly telling him to send Valentine again. Out of anyone who worked with their horses, Charlotte had the calmest spirit, and they needed Valentine to trust someone.

So Robbie worked the flag, yipped at the horse, and forced her back toward Charlotte, who still stood by the rail. She didn't move. Didn't hold a flag. Didn't call or encourage the horse in any way.

She simply stood there, and they wanted Valentine to give in, stop being so stubborn, and approach her like a lady.

The thrumming energy of the horse pounded through Beau's chest, almost creating a second heartbeat within him. She possessed a power that Charlotte seemed to respect and understand. Her approach was different from the last Stable Master they'd had here at the ranch—less about asserting dominance and more about mutual respect.

He had to admit, there was something magnetic about a woman who could hold her own in such a dance of wills. She didn't even seem to be bothered by it. And she hadn't moved, not so much as a shuffle or a sidestep.

She's standing for a while, he thought, an alarm starting a low wail in the back of his mind. He had no idea how long she'd been standing like that before he'd arrived, and he stopped watching Valentine and kept his gaze locked on Charlotte.

He'd told Pete, Squire, and Kenny about her heart condition, but no one else. Kenny stood on the other side of the circle, half on the fence and half off, and he didn't seem concerned about Charlotte at all.

Valentine huffed and shook her head, her ears going back for a moment. She retreated back toward Robbie, but she didn't want to be near him either. The horse tossed her head and kicked more dust up into the air as she faced Charlotte again.

She settled slightly in that she moved into a slow walk instead of the more excited pacing movement she'd been doing. And she headed straight for Charlotte.

"Nice and easy," Finn said, echoing the thoughts in Beau's head.

A bead of sweat ran down the side of Charlotte's face, but she made no move to wipe it away. Valentine continued toward her, the twelve-hundred-pound animal no lightweight. Horses could be bullies, just like people. They had huge heads and a lot of teeth, and since Valentine was new, and Beau had never worked with her himself, he had no idea how to read her mood.

They'd clearly tired her out enough for her to acquiesce, but he didn't know what would happen next. He couldn't even predict it.

Valentine moved right into Charlotte's shoulder, her head down, her nose right against the human. She almost looked like she was pressing Charlotte into the ground and refusing to let her move.

Beau's pulse picked up, and Robbie yipped at Valentine again. Charlotte reached up and pushed her back, forcing the horse to give her some room. She did, thankfully, and the cowboys here knew better than to make a ruckus or start clapping.

That would only spook Valentine—and honestly, Beau worried it would "freak out" Charlotte too.

Valentine crowded her again, and this time, Charlotte wavered on her feet. She looked away from the horse. She reached up with her hand, and Beau clearly saw her two fingers pressed together.

The sign for H.

She needed help.

He didn't waste a moment. Not even to breathe. Not to think. He jumped off the fence and hit the dirt running. "Robbie, get her away from Charlotte." He lifted both hands above his head as Robbie circled around behind Charlotte and lifted the flag to force Valentine back.

The horse huffed again and backed up, then turned and trotted as far from Robbie and Charlotte as she could get.

"All done for today," Beau said, his voice too loud to his own ears.

Charlotte turned toward him, a mighty frown on her face. That was his first hint that he'd done something wrong. "What was that?" she asked. "We finally got her over here."

"Robbie, can you get her back in her stall?"

"Sure thing, boss." He glanced over to Charlotte, a hint of worry in his eyes.

"No," Charlotte practically barked. "I need the time with her."

Beau did not want to have this conversation with her in front of everyone, but he would if he had to. "You...feeling okay?"

She blinked a few times, her eyelashes practically whipping up and down. "I'm fine, Beau."

He edged in closer to her and lowered his head. "You made the sign for help."

She stepped back, her ire like the heat of the sun. Even Beau wanted to put more distance between them. "I did not."

"I saw you."

She made the same huffing noise of displeasure that Valentine had made, and she grabbed the lead rope from the rail. "I'll get her back in her stall." She marched away from him, and she didn't sway or stumble.

Maybe she was okay.

But he'd seen her lift her hand. He knew he had.

Charlotte acted with an air of resilience and professionalism, but she threw Beau one more daggered look as she led Valentine out of the ring.

He watched her again, this time walking away from him and back toward the stable, a surge of protectiveness filling him from the bottom of his cowboy boots to the brim of his hat. He wanted to be the one who knew her signs, distressed or otherwise. He wondered if she'd ever admit to him that she was tired or overwhelmed or about to pass out.

She was such a strong woman, and Charlotte wouldn't want to admit any weakness. He suddenly understood the weight of responsibility Mason had been carrying all these years, and why he'd told Beau to keep an eye on Charlotte.

She won't admit it when she's not feeling well, he'd said.

His job wasn't just about running the ranch anymore; it was about caring for Charlotte, for seeing her through the storms of her health problems—because she would do the same for him. And in that quiet moment, with the dust settling and the cowboys dispersing and the sun dipping low, Beau realized that Charlotte wouldn't only become a fixture on his ranch. She was fast becoming the anchor in his life.

Oh, and he'd have to face her when they both returned to the cabin that night. He groaned inwardly, because they had a date on the schedule too, and he didn't want that marred by this afternoon's situation.

So, since he'd rather face her sooner rather than later, and he could work from the cabin, he returned there and stepped into the shower. He got dressed in date clothes for that evening, and he went through the schedule in the spare bedroom.

The moment he heard Charlotte come in, he abandoned his paperwork and headed out to the kitchen. She looked even dirtier than before, and he wasn't blind to how pale her face had become.

"Hey," he said.

She merely looked over to him as she hung up her hat.

"You made the sign for help," he said.

"I absolutely did not." She stepped toward him, her fingers

curling into fists once, twice, before she released them completely. "You embarrassed me out there, *and* you interrupted a perfectly good session."

"I did not embarrass you," he said. "No one thought anything of it."

"How could they not?" She shook her head and dodged by him to wash her hands in the kitchen sink.

Beau had laid out some cards this morning, but he wasn't sure how many more to deal tonight. "I'm never going to apologize for taking one of my guys out of a dangerous situation," he said.

"I was not *in* a dangerous situation." She pumped the soap dispenser way too many times, pink foam filling her palms twice over. "We'd worked for forty minutes to tire her out. She'd just come over to me."

"You stumbled."

"She pushed me!" Charlotte shook her head. "I'm not going to explain it." She washed all the way up to her elbows while Beau tried to find a better explanation for what he'd done. One that wasn't him over-reacting.

"Maybe we need a new hand symbol," he said.

"There were a dozen men there," she said. "All I needed to do was turn to Kenny and say, 'I need some help.' Case closed."

Beau moved in close beside her, the scent of lemons and sunshine coming from the soap. "But, Charlotte, will you do that?"

"Of course I will," she snapped at him, seemingly determined to be upset with him.

He slid his hand along her waist and drew her tight against his side. "Are you going to be mad that I worried about you?"

"Maybe," she said, clearly not willing to give in yet.

"I've pulled plenty of people out of a training ring before," he said. "I promise you, no one is going to think anything of it."

She dried her hands and rehung the towel over the handle on the oven. After drawing a big breath and then pushing it all out, she looked at him. "All right."

"I'm sorry," he said sincerely. "You do look pale. And tired." He didn't want to suggest they not go out that night, so he didn't. He wasn't sure he'd even be able to get his voice to say something so contrary to what he truly wanted.

"Lovely," she said dryly. "I'm going to go shower. We're still going to dinner tonight, right?"

"I want to," he said, his gaze dropping to her mouth. She didn't wear lipstick for the horses, and he wondered if she would for him.

"Then stop crowding into me and let me go shower." She shoved against his shoulder, and he fell back the same way Valentine had earlier that day. "Jeez, you're as bad as her." She gave him a quick smile that seemed to carry some flirty vibes as she brushed by him.

"We need a new hand signal," he called after her.

"No, we don't," she called back, and then her bathroom door slammed closed, putting the final punctuation mark on the conversation.

"Well." He looked down at Pepper and Ruby, who'd been witnesses to the whole thing. "I suppose that could've gone worse and it didn't."

Ruby responded by turning and trotting over to her food bowl. She sat down next to it and looked at him expectantly.

"Yeah, all right," he said. "I'll feed you two, but then Charlotte and I are going out, and I don't want you to be tearin' papers off my desk while I'm gone. Ya'hear?"

Oh, they both heard all right. Whether they'd listen to him and leave his stuff alone was another story.

Once the dogs were eating, Beau retreated to his bedroom and closed the door too. He wanted to "pick Charlotte up" for their date, and that meant knocking on the cabin door and waiting for her to come answer it.

So he needed to finish getting ready and then make himself scarce for the next hour. Then, he might just be on his last first date. The thought made his heartbeat quiver, and he headed out to go spend some time with his mini donkeys.

He could tell Jasper, Sprout, and Tilly all about Charlotte —oops, he already had. But they didn't know about that afternoon's incident in the training ring, and they'd want to hear about it. Plus, then it would be off his chest, and they could talk about the forthcoming date too.

Then, he'd be able to return to the cabin at the appointed time for his first date with stubborn, smart, sassy Charlotte Wisenhouer.

Chapter Twelve

Charlotte looked at the duo of dogs lying on the couch together. "Where did he go, huh?" She grinned at them and leaned over the couch to give Pepper a rub. The black lab immediately rolled onto his back while Ruby looked at her like she was still deciding if she wanted to be touched.

"You know you do," Charlotte said to the dog. "You always act so aloof, but I know you love me." She moved her hand over to Ruby, whose eyes lazily closed in bliss she tried not to show. Charlotte giggled at her. "See? You love it."

She needed the dogs to calm her before this date. Beau had said he'd leave the cabin so he could come pick her up "cowboy-gentleman proper," and she'd simply sent him a thumbs-up emoji and told herself she'd worry about her twisted emotions later.

Well, later had arrived, and she still didn't quite know why Beau made her blood vibrate in her veins. Or why Charlotte worried that this date could either make them or break them.

"Please don't let it break us," she said. Because if it did, she still had to live with this man. Live with him and work with him.

A knock sounded on the door, and Charlotte spun toward it. She couldn't remember the last time a man had come to the door to pick her up. She hadn't lived alone in so long, and it took her a few extra seconds to give her legs the command to go answer the door.

She yanked it open too hard, and it almost crashed into the wall behind it. Charlotte managed to stop it before her hand got smashed, and she looked straight at the epitome of cowboy perfection standing in front of her.

Almost.

A grin pulled across her face, and she said, "You have a little bit of mud on your face."

He immediately reached up to wipe it away, but it clung to his cheekbone and had dried in his beard. Charlotte found him adorable and handsome all in the same package, and she took a step closer. "Let me."

The moment sobered between them as she reached toward his left cheek with her right hand and gently brushed at the dried mud until it was gone. His hand settled on her waist, and Charlotte switched her gaze from his beard, which had a little bit of sexy gray growing in it, to meet his eyes.

"Charlotte," he whispered.

"You can't kiss me before the first date."

"No?"

"I'm feeling a little faint," she said, though she wasn't.

The flirtiness on his face vanished, but Charlotte giggled. "I'm kidding, Beau, but...." She stepped back, because her heart had started to pound like a big bass drum in a marching band. "I haven't kissed a man in a long, long time. I'm just a—"

"Nervous," he supplied for her.

"Yeah." She swallowed. "A little nervous, and I'd like to go out first." She leaned back into him and hugged him, thrilled when his arms came around her too. He sure knew how to hold a woman, and Charlotte wondered if maybe they should just cancel the drive to town and the loaded baked potato and spend the night dancing in each other's arms.

When she wasn't looking at him, it seemed easier to talk to him. "It just—sort of feels like we're doing things out of order, you know?"

"I've done things in all the right order," he murmured. "It's never worked out all that well for me, so I'm not too worried about the order of things."

"Well, I am."

"Okay, little bird," he whispered, his mouth right against her ear. The cascading way his breath slinked over her shoulder made her shiver. "So date first. Talking, and eating, and driving." He lilted to the right, almost dancing with her.

"Yeah." She swayed with him, glad she'd said something.

"It is a long drive to town," he said. "And I've been playing with the donkeys in the mud, and I'm starving."

"Can't have that," she said as she stepped out of his embrace. She laced her fingers through his and added, "You haven't introduced me to any donkeys. Where are those? Who takes care of them?"

"They're mine." He led her to the edge of the steps, and then turned back. "The door."

She hurried to close it, and then she joined him again. "You own donkeys?"

"Three of 'em," he said. "They're minis, and I got them from another cowboy. Gideon Walker? He loves 'em, but he can only have so many." He chuckled as he led her to the truck. "His wife won't let him have anymore, in fact."

Charlotte laughed too, and she got in the passenger seat and buckled her seatbelt. When Beau joined her, she said, "Felicity used to tell Mason that he couldn't buy another knife, so I get it."

"Mason's always loved his knives," Beau said with a smile.

"They don't take as much room as miniature donkeys," Charlotte said. "You never said where they are."

"There wasn't room in our stables or pastures. I've got them over at Courage Reins, in a nice little paddock with lots of their favorite grass."

"And some mud."

"They get a little sloppy when they're drinking is all."

"I want to meet them. I can't believe you've been holding out on me with mini donkeys."

"They're special to me," he said. "Not everyone gets to meet them." He turned onto the highway, and the ride turned smoother.

Charlotte giggled. "Really? You hold back your mini donkeys? Don't show them to your girlfriends until—when? The fourth date? Fifth?" She laughed again, and she couldn't remember laughing as much as she had before she came to live with Beau. To strike out on her own. That thought made her sober slightly, and she ducked her head and tucked her hair behind her ear.

She'd straightened it and clipped it back on the sides, but plenty still streamed over her shoulders.

"You don't reveal everything even on the first date," Beau said. "Surely you still have something we can talk about."

Charlotte looked out her window, the evening clouds in the sky as bright as they'd been during the day. Summer nights seemed to stretch on forever, and the sun wouldn't set for hours still. "I guess," she said.

"Go on then," he said.

"I know you've seen them."

Beau looked over to her, pure interest in his eyes. "Seen what?"

"My mismatched socks," she said. "You're just too polite to say anything about them."

He drove the truck for a few moments, and then he chuckled and said, "I've seen 'em."

"Yeah, you have."

He squeezed her hand and asked, "Why don't you match them up?"

"Why do something so futile?" she asked. "That's what I say. One of them always gets lost, and I just figured, I'd buy a whole bunch of the same kind. Same size. Same brand. All of that. And then, it wouldn't matter if one was white with purple stripes and one was black with orange. They fit the same, and no one sees 'em in my boots anyway."

"Oh, so I'm getting the foot-peep show at home, is that it?" He laughed, and Charlotte enjoyed the vibe in the truck. She enjoyed being with him, and she'd had no idea she could feel so comfortable with someone like him.

She'd honestly thought she'd never get married at all.

"Beau?" she asked.

"Mm?" He glanced over to her as he continued to drive.

"I—" She wanted to ask him about his dating experience, and perhaps a little about why he was almost forty—Mason's age—and had never been married. He seemed hard-working and responsible, though she had heard him laughing and chatting with his video game friends.

He laughed easily, and everyone seemed to love him—Charlotte included.

"I haven't dated anyone in a few years," she said. She rolled her head, stretching her neck, and sighed. "Fine, a few is an under-exaggeration. I haven't had a serious relationship with a man, ever, and I haven't dated anyone in oh, eight years."

He nodded, suddenly serious too. "I feel that."

"Oh, come on. What I just said can't be true for you."

"I mean, maybe not." He smiled over to her as the first houses in town came into view. "I dated a lot in my twenties and early thirties. A lot, a lot." He shifted in his seat and pulled his hand away from hers. She wasn't sure what that meant, and his nervousness bled into her.

"I wasn't serious about anything but having a good time. As I got older, I realized I wasn't sure how to really date seriously, so I made a lot of mistakes."

She'd suspected he'd had a lot more experience than her, and that only made the thought of kissing him even more terrifying. More exciting. And exponentially more horrifying for her if she turned out to be terrible at kissing cowboys.

"I got better at it," he said quietly. "But since then, I've never found anyone I can see myself spending the rest of my life with."

"I see."

"I haven't been out with anyone for about three years now. Maybe four."

Relief she hadn't known she needed slipped through her. "So maybe I'm not out of my league," she said.

"Of course you're not," he said. "I'm only older than you, not better."

"Yeah, well, with Mason, being older means being better."

"Yeah, well," he drawled, mimicking her. "I'm not Mason." Their eyes met, and everything in the world turned into a sizzling, foaming chemistry experiment. He had to feel that too, and by the darkening edge in his eyes, he did. Oh, he did.

"All right, then," she said. "I'm ready for this baked potato." That lightened the mood, and Beau smiled. Charlotte did too, and since Felicity liked cooking, she hadn't eaten out much. And because she was new in town, there were a great many restaurants for Charlotte to sample.

Beau chuckled and pulled into the restaurant parking lot. Charlotte wasn't sure what they had to talk about, but she'd never struggled to be with Beau, so she put it from her mind. He got out to come around and open her door, and in the moment his door closed, the sweetest feeling of peace flowed through her.

"This is okay," she whispered to herself. Beau rounded the

front of the truck, his head down, his cowboy hat hiding most of his face. Her heartbeat clanged through her chest at the mere thought of kissing that cowboy.

Just as quickly as the nerves came, God quieted them. *It's okay*, she thought, wondering if the thoughts were hers or not. *I am with you.*

Charlotte had often felt that Jesus walked with her, and tears filled her eyes at the reminder that while she did scary things—like dating Beau Peterson—she didn't have to be alone. That she wasn't alone.

He opened her door, and Charlotte swiped at her face quickly, just to make sure no tears had escaped. "Ready for your loaded baked potato, little bird?"

She took a quick breath and said, "So ready."

* * *

"I had no idea it would take that long to eat at a steakhouse," Charlotte said as Beau made the turn from the smooth highway and onto the well-groomed dirt road that belonged to Three Rivers Ranch. "Will you still get up and do your morning live-stream?"

"I never miss the live-stream," he said. "Unless I'm so sick, I literally can't get out of bed." He squeezed her hand. "It's fine, Charlotte. I knew we'd be out for a while."

"Plus the drive," she said, still worried. "It's dark already, Beau."

"Charlotte," he said. "It's fine. I was thinking we might

even go for a walk once we get back to the cabin. The moon's real bright tonight."

She looked over to him. She felt like she'd sat on fire ants, and everything itched. She needed to get out of this truck right now, and she figured he was only driving about thirty miles an hour. She could jump and roll at that speed, couldn't she?

"You better talk to me," he said in that powerful voice he had when working with cattle, horses, and men.

"I'm okay." She looked away and folded her arms. "I'm just worried that it's so late."

He made the wide, arcing turn and the ranch came into view. The two homesteads, the big Courage Reins building, with Bowman's Breeds on her left-hand side.

"The energy with you changed," he said. "What is it?"

She knew exactly what it was, and she'd be stunned if he didn't too. So she didn't say anything.

"It's your heart, isn't it?" he asked, and he had that teasing quality in his voice. "It's growing and giving room to fall in love with me, isn't it?" He chuckled and added, "Don't admit it, okay? Just let it happen, sweetheart."

Charlotte looked over to him, wondering how he could joke about this.

"Or maybe you're just real nervous about kissin' me," he said. "So I'll just say right now—I'm not going to kiss you tonight."

Ice filled her chest, and she struggled to breathe against it. "You're not?"

"No, ma'am," he said. "So stop worrying, and let's go back to having a good time."

So easy for him to say. He went down past the barns and stables and around the administration building to their private parking against the back of the cabin. She didn't wait for him to come open her door for her, and instead, she met him at the corner of the truck and let him take her hand in his.

"I love the moon," he said, looking up into the sky at the gentle giant of an orb. "She's almost full tonight, but I think she's got a sliver left to go." Beau looked at her, and Charlotte stopped admiring the yellow glow of the moon to meet his eyes.

He didn't hesitate, and he didn't say anything. He simply lifted his hand and slid it along her jaw, then around to the back of her neck. He leaned down and touched his mouth to hers in a sweet kiss.

Beau stayed there for only a moment, barely long enough for the burn to start tingling in her lips. Then he pulled away, whispered, "Sorry I lied," and kissed her like he meant it.

Chapter Thirteen

Beau had imagined kissing Charlotte. Plenty of times. When he should've been getting paperwork ready, or paying more attention to what was going on with the vaccinations of their cattle dogs.

When he'd felt her mood shift so violently, he'd told himself sternly that he would not kiss her tonight. Not if it was going to make everything inside her into an earthquake. He'd told himself he could look up at the moon, and hold her hand as they walked along the fields of alfalfa, the scent of the good earth, and the dark sky above them.

But one look at her in the moonlight, and he'd just acted. He'd done what he knew how to do, and oh, kissing Charlotte in real life instead of in his fantasies was a hundred times better than anything he could've dreamed up.

She matched him stroke for stroke, and he cradled her face in both of his hands, feeling something shift powerfully inside him. He breathed in and pulled back. Charlotte edged forward, and he touched his lips to hers again, so much inside him now soaring as high as the moon above him.

He pulled away further and tucked Charlotte against his chest. He didn't mind looking a woman in the eye after he kissed her, but he thought Charlotte would like a few moments to herself. She sighed and nestled right into the space inside his arms he hadn't realized was shaped exactly like her.

"Wow," he whispered. "You're really good at kissing for not having done it for a while."

She jerked up and blinked at him. He grinned at her, and she caught on to his teasing a moment too late. "You're such a tease." She pushed against his chest with one palm while simultaneously fitting herself back against him. "Do you really want to go for a walk?"

"Not really," he said. "I can see the moon from here." He glanced up to it again, and it was so bright, it actually hurt his eyes a little. "Do I get another date?"

"Mm, yes," she said.

"Maybe we can take the horses out to the stream and have sandwiches tomorrow after work," he said. "Saves us the drive in and back."

"If I can take New Yorker, it's a deal."

He chuckled, because she had talked about the pretty bay several times in the two weeks she'd been working at the ranch.

"And." She pushed away from him again and searched his face. "You're not picking me up like you did tonight."

"Deal on both counts," he said. "Now, let's go see what the dogs have torn up and then get to bed."

"You keep saying your dogs are naughty when you're gone, but I've never seen it."

He turned around and tucked her against his side as they made their way around the side of the house to the front steps. "Pepper has a wolfish streak every now and then," he said. "You stay around long enough, you'll see it."

He opened the door to the cabin and guided her inside first. Charlotte took three steps, maybe enough to go behind the couch that he'd positioned facing the wall to his right.

Then she stopped abruptly and sucked in a breath. He entered and closed the door behind him, asking, "What is it?" Beau eased right in behind her, easily sliding his hands along her waist as he looked over her shoulder.

In front of him, the white ceramic bowl that usually held apples and oranges lay on the floor, one big piece broken off and leaving a macabre smile left in the dish. Not a single piece of fruit could be seen, but Beau scanned the floor in all directions, searching.

He glanced over to the couch, where Pepper and Ruby usually lay while he was out. Not a dog in sight.

"Told you," he said as he stepped past her. He whistled through his teeth as he bent to pick up the bowl. "Come on out, guys." He retrieved the broken piece of the fruit bowl and looked down the hall as nails clicked against the wood.

"Mm hm." He put everything on the counter and cocked his hip as Ruby led the way toward him, clutching a bright green apple in her mouth.

* * *

"She just texted to say she's on her way," Beau said as he brushed this hand along Tilly's flank. He loved her spotted complexion, and he'd just finished giving the white donkey with gray patterns running along her sides a bath. "You're all ready to meet her."

He'd put off bringing Charlotte over to the paddock where he kept his minis, only because they'd been busy on the ranch. And spending time together every evening. She was really good with horses, and Beau really liked that. Not all of his previous girlfriends had been able to saddle two horses and bring one to him while he finished up his day's work, and he'd super enjoyed that.

They'd ridden out to the stream and eaten sandwiches, and the next night, he'd made breakfast burritos for the two of them and they'd sat on the back deck and watched the full moon rise over the gorgeous Texas landscape.

Because they lived together, Beau didn't have to try very hard to see her. She hadn't asked to come with him in the mornings for his sunrise live-stream, and he hadn't invited her along.

Just because they lived together didn't mean he needed to rush into having her in every part of his life. Heck, it had taken another week since their first date—and their first kiss—for him to suggest she come meet the donkeys.

"So here we are." He grinned at his gray donkey with the black face—Jasper—as he trotted away from the gate and toward Pepper. Sometimes Jasper liked to play pretend and act like he could smell the same things the canines could. No matter what, he liked them best, and he palled around with them whenever Beau came to the paddock.

He chuckled at the sight of Jasper's little kick—his indication of excitement—the warmth of the summer evening sun casting long shadows across the paddock. "You're quite the character, Jasper," Beau said with a shake of his head. Tilly looked over to Jasper and the dogs, and Sprout ambled over to see what the fuss was about, her gentle eyes filled with curiosity.

"Yeah, he's off with the dogs. You wanna go? Charlotte's gonna be here soon." Sprout didn't seem to care about becoming a dog, and she wandered a few paces away and bent her head to get more to eat. Of course. Out of the trio of mini donkeys, she ate the most.

A soft hum of an engine announced Charlotte's arrival before she even stepped into view. Beau straightened, his heart finding a new, strange rhythm at the thought of her meeting his cherished donkeys. It wasn't just an introduction; it was sharing a part of his soul that he kept hidden from most.

"You invited her," he reminded himself. "You can't hide them forever." Like the video games and the sunrise livestreams, if he really wanted to be with someone long-term, they'd have to learn everything about him. Even his semi-fascination with miniature donkeys.

A vehicle door closed with a thud, and moments later, Charlotte's figure came into sight. She had changed from her work clothes of men's shirts and jeans and into something more relaxed—a simple summer dress in lavender that would make her eyes shine like amethysts in full sunlight.

Her hair was still pulled back in a loose ponytail, strands framing her sun-kissed face, as she ducked her head shyly and came toward him.

"There's a gate right there," he said. "It's unlocked."

"Do you ever lock it?" she called, reaching up to unlatch the gate.

"Absolutely, I do," he said. "These guys are cute, but Sprout thinks she should have free range of the Texas Panhandle."

"Sorry, I'm late," she said, her smile reaching her eyes when she turned after closing the gate behind her. "Had to make sure the new foal was settled for the night."

"How's Peanut?" he asked. The mare had been an anxious mother in the past forty-eight hours, and Charlotte hadn't come in until ten o'clock last night, as she'd been out in the barn, trying to get Peanut to settle enough to leave her with her foal for the night.

"She's great," Charlotte said. "First-time moms are always a little jumpy." She looked down at Tilly. "How are you, princess?"

"That there's Tilly," he said as she started to stroke the donkey's neck. "She loves bath day." He indicated Sprout, who looked up somewhat lazily. "That's Sprout. Come on, girl. Come say hello."

"She'll come say hello for this." Charlotte reached into her pocket and pulled out a banana. Beau shouldn't have been surprised, but he sort of was. They hadn't talked about mini donkeys or what they liked, but most of them went nuts for a banana.

In fact, Sprout loved them so much, she made a high-pitched bray that almost sounded like a cry. Like she was in pain.

Charlotte laughed as she peeled the banana. Tilly crowded in close, and Ruby and Pepper, sensing the excitement, darted back to Charlotte in a welcoming frenzy. Of course.

"Guys," Beau said, moving to stand in front of Charlotte. "Mind your manners. It's a banana, for crying out loud."

Charlotte giggled as she patted the dogs, and then she broke off a chunk of banana. "Heya, Tilly." She spoke with a natural ease in her voice that soothed him as well as the donkeys. "You're so pretty."

Tilly extended her muzzle toward Charlotte's hand while Sprout expressed her displeasure at not being fed first with another braying cry.

"Sprout," he chastised, but the donkey didn't care at all. "She's a bit of an attention-seeker, and she loves to eat."

Charlotte's laugh flowed easily from her, and Beau liked the casualness of it. He liked how easy everything between them had become. "I think I can relate to that," she said playfully.

She fed Sprout and then Jasper, and then she went around again and gave each donkey a second bite of banana, reserving two chunks—one for each dog. She spoke to them like people too, which warmed his heart. In fact, as Beau watched, a deep sense of contentment settled in his chest.

He hadn't brought anyone to meet his minis in so long, and it felt good. Right. Easy.

With the banana gone, the donkeys wandered off to find

greener grass, and Beau led Charlotte over to a quiet spot on a couple of hay bales. Pepper sighed and circled as he lay at Beau's feet, and he fell in love with his life all over again.

"Thanks for letting me come meet them," she said.

"Figured you'd have to sooner or later," he said. "And now you know why I like to come visit them when things get crazy."

She adjusted her hand in his and gazed at the donkeys with softness in her expression. "Do I?"

"Can't you feel it?" He shifted closer to her, and she leaned back into his chest with a sigh of contentment. "There's something about this place—these animals—that's soothing. I can talk to them, and they listen to all my hopes, fears, and prayers. I feel like God's closer out here, in the simplicity of green grass, and hay bales, and clean mini donkeys."

She turned to him, her gaze sparking with energy. "I feel that. There's a peace here that you can't find just anywhere. It's like you can hear Him in the quiet."

He nodded, finding courage in her shared sentiment. "Exactly. It's where I find strength, and when things are crazy on the ranch, or I feel unsettled, I come here. You sing to the horses in the stable, and I bathe my minis."

She grinned at him and said, "I don't sing to them every day."

"I still haven't heard any singing in the stables," he teased.

"It's like you saying the dogs are naughty when you're gone," she said. "You stick around long enough, it'll happen." She faced the pasture again, and Beau did the same. They hadn't eaten dinner yet, and his hunger status would probably embarrass him soon enough.

Thankfully, his stomach didn't growl immediately, and he enjoyed holding Charlotte in his arms.

"There's a saying my mom used to say," she said. "'Faith is not about everything turning out okay; it's about being okay no matter how things turn out.'"

Beau let the words roll around in his head, trying to make them line up. No, things didn't always turn out okay, but sometimes, it was about the learning, the growth, that happened as he went through something hard.

"I like that," he said.

"Being here with you, with them." She gestured at the paddock and the donkeys. Ruby had bedded down with Pepper, and they both watched the minis. "It feels like everything will be okay, and that if it's not, *I'll* still be okay. It's that kind of faith."

A smile tugged at his lips, one that was mirrored by Charlotte. He enjoyed the physical closeness between them, as he hadn't had it in a while, but the emotional bond tying him to Charlotte was just as important.

Shared beliefs. Mutual respect. A burgeoning love that promised to grow as steady and true as the land they both cherished. Could he even hope for that? After so many years of striking out?

He'd been praying for such a thing—for such a companion —and as the sun slipped lower in the sky, Charlotte seemed to etch herself right on the surface of his heart.

And he hoped she'd stay there forever, burrow deeper, and become part of him permanently.

* * *

"He did what?" Beau watched Squire pace in his office, sure his ears had malfunctioned.

"He joined the Army." Squire finally came to a stop and looked out the window. "Kelly's throwing a good-bye party, of course. Can you text out the details to everyone?"

"Of course I can." Beau didn't want to leave the office, though, because the unrest stomped along the walls and coated the ceiling. Squire's unrest.

What should I say here? he prayed, hoping God would give him the right words. Beau didn't have any kids, and certainly not a twenty-year-old leaving for Basic Training in a couple of days.

"Finn's a good man," Beau said. "He's been working real hard this summer, and I can't imagine he won't do the same in the Army."

"Yeah," Squire said. "I just know what that's like, and I worry." He faced Beau. "I can't be worried at home, because that upsets Kelly, and well, I have to pace it all out here." He flashed a smile in Beau's direction, not really looking at him.

"What can I do for you?" Beau asked.

That got Squire to look over to him. "I—don't know."

"I imagine there's not much to be done," Beau said quietly. "I'll pray for you. Did you call the pastor and put his name on the prayer roll?"

Squire shook his head, something storming across his face that Beau hardly ever saw on the strong, capable, hard-working boss's face.

"I'll do it," Beau said. Heck, he'd put not only Finn's name on the prayer list, but Squire's and Kelly's too. All of their children, who were probably worried about their older brother entering the Army.

Squire nodded just one time. "Thank you, Beau."

He nodded too, and said, "All right, well, I'll text out the details about the lunch, and I'm sure everyone who can be will be there." With that, he left Squire's corner office and headed into his.

With deft fingers, he sent the message, and then he sank into his chair and looked up to the ceiling. "Dear Jesus," he whispered. "Bless the Ackermans in any way they need it. Envelop them in protection and safety, both here on the ranch and wherever life takes Finn."

Texts poured in. Beau ran through them quickly, and then he sent another message. *Yeah, you guys know how Kelly and Squire are. Providing everything for all of us here. Let's bring them all we can for this, okay? Flowers, cards, food, and all our best attitudes and prayers.*

He sent that and added, *If you get something specific, put it here so we don't double up.*

Then he called Holly Ann, who answered with, "What's up, Beau? Ordering your own birthday cake this year?"

He chuckled and said, "Maybe, but not today. No, what I need from you and Three Cakes, Holly Ann, is a schedule and price sheet for those family meals you were talking about."

"Family meals," she said.

"I know your baby is due soon, but...." He might as well tell her. The entire town of Three Rivers would rally around the Ackermans once they found out Finn had entered the Army.

"Kelly and Squire are going to need them for a little bit. Finn's going into Basic Training next week."

Holly Ann pulled in a breath and then said, "I'll get it set up."

"I want to pay for it," Beau said.

She scoffed, and he could just see her swinging her head, her dark hair moving with it. "Not a chance. Thanks for letting me know, Beau."

"Holly Ann—"

"I'll get the word out to the Glovers and text Kelly so she knows when I'll be bringing her meals. They've got three other kids?" She seemed to be musing to herself, and Beau recognized a runaway train when he saw one.

So he left her to her muttering, and he went back to praying for his friends who had become his family.

Chapter Fourteen

Charlotte had never seen so many people gathered outside of church, a funeral, or a wedding.

In fact, the number of men, women, and children currently crowding into the barn where Bennett had gotten married seemed to be twice as many people as any of those things.

Squire and Kelly's son, Finn, was leaving Three Rivers Ranch for service in the United States Army. Charlotte had met Finn, of course. He worked with her in the stables quite often, in fact.

He was tall and charming and young—and dating a pretty blonde his age named Edith. She was planning to go to France for an au pair job, and apparently Finn had decided his path included military service.

He also hadn't told anyone that—not even his parents—until a few days ago. Kelly's party-planning skills shouted from the rafters of the barn, where camouflage streamers hung down and chatter and party music lifted up.

"It's a buffet," Beau said, his hand in hers tight. She didn't want to lose him in this crowd, because this was way more than just the normal Three Rivers crowd.

"Come meet some of the Glovers," he said, taking her away from the food. The people thinned enough that she didn't have to brush past anyone here, and Beau led her over to a few couples. "Preach."

One man turned toward him and immediately stepped in to hug him. "Beau, brother, hey."

Beau stepped back smiling and indicated Charlotte. "This is Charlotte," he said. "Charlotte, this is Preacher Glover, his cousin Ward Glover, and the owner of Shiloh Ridge Ranch, Bear Glover."

"That's a lot of Glovers," Charlotte said, letting herself sparkle as much as possible. She shook all of their hands, and listened while they introduced their wives.

Charlie, Dot, and Sammy. They had little children with them, and by the time those names were said, they'd started to blur in Charlotte's head.

She did know one thing, though. "You play games with Preacher and Ace," she said.

"Yeah." A smile bloomed on Beau's face. "He's around here somewhere, I'm sure."

"He went to get a gluten-free tortilla wrap," Bear said. "As if they'd run out of those."

A beat of silence followed, wherein Charlotte wasn't sure if he was trying to be funny or if he'd literally just growled the words.

Then Sammy said, "Don't be a grizzly, Bear."

"I'm just sayin'," Bear said. "No one's going to take a gluten-free tortilla when there's a perfectly glutened one available." He took a little girl from his wife, and the child softened the cowboy considerably. He even smiled at her.

Preacher started to laugh, as did Beau, and Charlotte decided it was okay to smile too.

Beau stepped back to expand the circle as more cowboys arrived. "Hey, you." He grabbed onto one of them, the one with the darkest features, darkest hair, deepest eyes.

"Charlotte," he said. "This is Jeremiah Walker. The Walker boys own Seven Sons Ranch."

"Great to meet you," Charlotte said, shaking his hand. And he had six brothers. The families here...she'd never seen so many of them.

She and Beau managed to talk to at least fifty people before they got food, and then she sat down at a table with Bennett and Ellie, Rhett and Evelyn Walker, and Ace and Holly Ann Glover.

A feeling of acceptance streamed through her, and she noted that she was at this party as part of a couple—and she liked that. She glanced at Beau, who pressed a kiss to her temple before he turned back to his food, looked across the table, and picked up his non-gluten wrap.

"So," he said. "Rhett, you workin' on any cases right now?"

Before he could answer, a man said into a mic, "Thank you, everyone, for coming out to Three Rivers tonight."

It took a couple of seconds for the chatter to die down, and Charlotte took a bite of her wrap as she located Squire with the mic in his hand. Kelly stood next to him, an anxious look on her face, and Finn stood beside her.

Libby, Mike, and Sam—the rest of the Ackerman clan—stood there with them, and Squire looked down the row of his family, and Beau settled his arm around Charlotte's shoulders.

He leaned in close and whispered, "This is hard on them."

"I can see that," she said.

"Squire served in the Army for a handful of years," Beau said. "You've seen his limp, right? His tank got hit."

Charlotte had seen the man's limp, and she'd actually taken strength from it. No one treated him differently. No one told him he couldn't do something.

And she realized that out here, on this ranch, no one was limiting her either.

* * *

A week or so later, once Finn had left and ranch life had settled back to normal, Charlotte pulled up to her brother's house. While it looked like a very large farmhouse on the outside, she knew it was a high-end mansion on the inside. She sighed heavily, the weight of the secrets she carried keeping her in the driver's seat.

She hadn't been off Three Rivers Ranch and back here for Sunday dinner since she'd moved out, and it had been five weeks now. Felicity had been calling and texting a lot more this past week, so Charlotte had driven herself to church instead of going with Beau, and she'd made the quick drive southeast of town after the sermon.

She did miss the kids, and she laughed as the front door opened and all four of them came spilling out. That got her to get out of the SUV, and she hurried toward them, gathering them all to her the way a mother hen welcomed home her chicks.

"My babies," she said. "How are you? What have you been doing? Are you ready for school to start?"

They all talked over one another, and Charlotte seemed to be able to hear each of them and their concerns and excitement. School started tomorrow, in fact, and she suddenly remembered she'd gotten gifts for each of them.

"Oh, Ella, grab that brown bag off my back seat, would you?"

The teenager went to do that, and Charlotte herded the rest of the children up the steps. Felicity waited for her on the porch, and she pulled Charlotte into a hug. "Mm, it's so good to see you." She stepped back and held her at arm's length. "To know you're alive."

"Of course I'm alive." Charlotte shook her head as she rolled her eyes. "I text you all the time." She continued inside, where the scent of freshly baked bread lingered.

"Mason's grilling tonight," she said. "Ella helped me with the potato salad, and I made rolls, of course."

"It smells great."

"Did you want to make strawberry jam for real?" Felicity asked. "I got all the stuff, but it's okay if you don't want to."

"I do," Charlotte said. "Beau doesn't eat jam, and I had to resort to buying it from the grocery store."

Felicity blinked at her like such a thing wasn't even possible. "We'll make sure to get it done today. I just—no jam?"

Charlotte giggled and shook her head. "No jam."

"I don't even see how he's Texan."

"He's from New Mexico," Charlotte said.

"Sounds like you two are getting along." Felicity led the way into the kitchen and opened a cupboard to get down plates. "Garrett, Kennedy, time to set the table. Alice, you're on napkin duty."

Ella came inside and put Charlotte's brown bag on the counter. "I'll go help Daddy with the chicken."

"Take the platter," Felicity said after her, and Ella turned back to grab it before she headed outside. Charlotte got out silverware for the kids to use to set the table, and she wasn't expecting Felicity to go back to questioning her.

"Sounds like you and Beau are getting along," Felicity said in a forced casual way.

Charlotte jerked her head up. "Uh, yeah. He's nice. Great." She pressed her eyes closed. Nice? Great? What a disaster her mouth had just walked into.

Because Felicity knew her, and she'd heard the lame words Charlotte had just used. "Char...."

"We're dating," she said, the words just flying from her. "And I know it's a little crazy, but it doesn't feel that crazy to me when I'm there in the cabin with him, and I'm the one who has to handle it, so it's fine." She glanced over to Garrett as he picked up the stack of forks, and Charlotte's eyes moved to the back door to see if Mason was coming inside.

"I know Mason's going to flip his lid," Charlotte said. "But he doesn't get to decide. I like Beau. He's sweet, and hand-some, and hard-working. He's got these mini donkeys that he loves, and all his cowboys do whatever he asks, because they respect and like him."

"He sounds nice," Felicity teased, and Charlotte's pulse relaxed.

"Could you tell Mason?"

"Heavens, no," Felicity said. "Believe it or not, your brother just wants what's best for you."

"Yeah, sure," Charlotte said as the back door opened. Ella came inside with a platter of grilled, glistening-with-barbecue-sauce chicken, which meant Mason wouldn't be far behind. "I just wish he wouldn't growl so much in the process."

Felicity laughed, but she knew she'd married a grumpy cowboy. Somehow, he softened for her, and they did love each other fiercely.

"Chicken's off," Mason said as he came inside with another plate, this one piled with steak. "We're ready."

"So are we," Felicity said, taking a moment to keep her gaze locked on Charlotte before she faced her husband. "Remember, we haven't seen Char for weeks, and we don't want to scare her off again."

"You didn't scare me off before," Charlotte said, though her pulse did drop to her toes with one look at her brother.

His eyebrows had already drawn themselves into a V, and he looked from Felicity to her. "Scare her off? I don't scare her off."

"Do too," Felicity said. "Now, everyone come sit down. It's time to eat. Alice, just bring the rest over. It's time to eat."

The kids started to gather around the table, most of them asking about the steak and whether they could have it or not. But Mason stayed in the kitchen, the plate of meat between them. "Charlotte?"

"I'm dating Beau." She looked straight at him, feeling stronger than she had in a long time. Her heart beat steadily, the way she imagined it did for someone without a health problem. "It's going pretty great, actually, and I would appreciate it if you didn't ruin this for me."

His mouth dropped open, and oh, a furious fire raged in this eyes.

"Babe, bring the steak over," Felicity said. "We're eating." She took the plate from him and looked at Charlotte. "Come on, you two. We can talk when we're not hangry." She nudged Mason, who startled and looked at his wife.

Felicity took the steak over to the table, and Mason watched her for a moment. Then he met Charlotte's gaze again. "I'm not going to ruin anything for you, Char," he said. "If you like Beau, great."

Charlotte gave a mirthless laugh. "It's not great, and you know it." She turned and moved over to the table, bending to get a napkin Alice had dropped at some point.

"But I'm not going to ruin it for you," Mason called after her.

We'll see, she thought, and then she prayed with everything in her that nothing would ruin the good thing she had going with Beau. He was the first man who hadn't treated her like she was broken and couldn't do anything, and she appreciated that so much more than she'd even known she would.

As Ella prayed over the food, Charlotte added her own silent prayer that dinner would go well, that Mason would let this drop, and that she could take home some of Felicity's delicious strawberry jam for her handsome boyfriend to try.

* * *

Exhaustion pounded behind Charlotte's eyes as she moved down the row in the stable. She had three more stalls to clean, and then she'd be done for today. At least for a couple of hours, and she could have Kenny do the evening feeding tonight.

The kids had been in school for a week, and she'd been getting texts every night about their teachers and how they'd settled in so well. She missed them so much, but she didn't want to go back even a year in time to where she'd been last August.

She led Bolt out of his stall, and the pretty Palomino plodded along behind her without complaint. He wouldn't, because she'd put him in a great pasture where he'd get to be outside with his friends. She made that trip two more times to get the other horses out of the stable, and then she wheeled the wheelbarrow down the aisle to the last three stalls.

Her back ached, and by the time she finished, the teeth on the right side of her face actually throbbed with their own heartbeat.

And Charlotte knew she was in trouble.

She left the last stall and closed the door behind her. But she didn't try to take the waste out to the bin or get back to the cabin. Instead, she moved as quickly as she dared down the hall to the small office.

She ducked inside and took a seat in the only chair in the room. It sat at a table where she kept her notes and files, and she put her head down and breathed in slowly, trying to control her emotions so they didn't add to her sudden stress.

Something told her to call Beau, but she didn't have the energy to even reach for her phone. With her eyes closed, she started to hum to herself. A lullaby her mother used to sing to her when she was a little girl, and then in the hospital when they had to wait for tests.

She knew the words, but forming them took too much from her, so Charlotte just hummed while she rested. She didn't feel like she was going to pass out, but Beau would want to know about this situation anyway.

Charlotte tried to remember when she'd last eaten or drank, and she'd had lunch. She'd had a granola bar an hour ago, but she probably hadn't gotten enough water that day. She lifted her head and got to her feet slowly, really paying attention to the things that hurt.

She didn't normally suffer from headaches, so this didn't seem related to her heart condition. No, she'd just overworked herself today. Her big water bottle waited out in the stable, on the shelf across from the last stall.

After she made it there, she took a long drink, already feeling slightly better. What she really needed was some food, some painkillers, and an ice pack for her lower jaw, which still ached as if she'd had dental work done that day.

But she still had three horses to bring back in and all the

waste she'd pulled out of their stalls to dispose of. She moved down to the stall where a tall, reddish-black horse had already been out and had a clean stall.

She started to sing to Bronco as she put both hands on either side of his head and stroked down his neck, using the horse to help stabilize her. She smiled at the equine, who had a calm, gentle spirit. Bronco worked with the clients at Courage Reins, not with the cowboys at Three Rivers Ranch, and Charlotte could tell a difference between the therapy horses and the others.

The ranch owned many great cutting horses too, and they had to have a certain attitude to work with a cowboy and separate cattle from the herd. Charlotte loved watching cutting competitions, and she needed to ask Beau if any of the horses here had ever competed in such an event.

"You're a good boy," she said to Bronco, and then she moved down to Woodstock and started singing to him. She calmed too, and while she didn't start to feel better, she started to think she could finish her job for the day without asking for help.

Then, as she moved down to Valentine, her legs shook about the knees. As she sang, she got out her phone and created a group text with Beau and Kenny. *I need help in the third stable. I'm not feeling well, and I'm not done with the work.*

On my way, Beau said instantly, before Charlotte had even sung the next note in her song. Satisfied that she'd done the right thing, but with her heart hanging heavily in her chest, she looked at Valentine and kept singing to her.

She sensed Beau as he approached, because he came with all the energy of thunder and lightning. And he didn't pause a distance from her, but moved right into her, his arm sliding around her waist. "You're still standing."

"I don't think I'm going to pass out," she said. "I just have this awful headache, and I need to go home."

"I can finish," Kenny said, his footsteps coming closer. "Just the last three stalls?"

"They're done." She looked over to him. "I just have to take out the wheelbarrow and bring the horses back in."

"They can stay out too," Beau said. "No big deal."

"It's hot," Charlotte said. "They were out all morning too."

"I'll get 'em back in," Kenny said. "I'm done with the barn repairs."

Beau nodded at him, and Kenny went past them to get the wheelbarrow. They'd have to move for him to get out, and Charlotte let Beau keep her hand in his tightly as they went outside.

The sunshine made her squint, and a strong blast of pain shot behind her eyes. She groaned, and Beau glanced at her with a fierce look in his eyes. "Charlotte."

"I just need to take some medicine and lie down," she said.

"Then let's get you home."

Home. The word echoed in her head, and she hadn't felt completely at home anywhere, not like she did here. Not like she did at Beau's side.

He led her inside and right down the hall to her bedroom. "I'll bring you some painkillers." Before he left, he pulled her curtains closed, and Charlotte didn't bother to change her clothes. She took off her boots and lay back on her pillows, and when Beau brought her a bottle of water and some pills, she drank and took them readily.

"My teeth hurt," she said. "Can you bring me an ice pack?"

"Your *teeth* hurt?"

"When I get really bad headaches, it goes all the way into my teeth," she said, her eyes falling closed again. "And Beau?"

"What else do you need, little bird?"

She smiled at the beautiful pet name he had for her. At first, she hadn't liked it much, though she'd enjoyed how it rumbled in his voice. But birds were weak—or so she'd thought. But over the past several weeks, she'd realized that Beau didn't call her "little bird" because he found her weak.

He did it because he cherished her.

"Something to eat, please," she said. "Something easy. Just so the pills don't upset my stomach."

"Pizza coming right up." He left the room then, and Charlotte exhaled out and tried to relax. For some reason, she didn't mind when Beau took care of her, but she'd have been annoyed if she'd had to call her brother or her mother. She wasn't sure what the difference was, only that it existed.

When Beau returned, he brought the scent of marinara and pepperoni with him, and he sat on the edge of the bed while she scooted up and leaned against the wall to eat.

"I finally got to hear you sing to the horses," he said.

"And? What did you think?"

"I think you're the most beautiful woman in the world." Beau grinned at her, and she couldn't quite tell if he was joking or not. A flirt, he was, for sure.

"Because I sang a lullaby to a horse?"

"Because you sang a lullaby to a horse," he confirmed, and he certainly didn't seem to be joking. He threaded his fingers through hers. "You have a beautiful voice, and I'm sorry you aren't feeling well."

"I'm fine, really," she said. "Just a long day, and I have a headache."

"So, do you want to come lie on the couch and ice your teeth? I'll hold you and you can sing me your horse lullabies."

Charlotte grinned at him and reached out to cradle his face in one palm. His beard was soft and prickly at the same time, and he leaned into her touch as if he craved it. "Can you just hold me right here?"

Surprise crossed Beau's face, but he got up and went around to the other side of the bed. He lay down, and Charlotte scooted back down and pressed her back into his chest as his arms came around her. "Mm, this is nice."

She repositioned the ice pack so it covered her jaw and cheek, and she only grunted slightly when Ruby and Pepper joined them by jumping up onto the bed and finding spots near their feet.

Dozing, she finally felt every muscle in her body soften. So she couldn't be sure if she heard Beau whisper, "I'm falling in love with you, little bird," or not. Perhaps she simply wanted to hear it, or perhaps it had happened in her dreams.

No matter what, she liked hearing him say it, and she started wondering if she was falling in love with him too.

Chapter Fifteen

Beau couldn't wait to get back to the ranch—and take a shower. He'd been out on the roundup for too long, and he wasn't sure his soon-to-be-forty-year-old body could take another night sleeping on the ground.

Thankfully, he wouldn't have to, as the cattle and the horses had picked up the pace, apparently smelling the feast Kelly and her team of cooks had put together. Someone up ahead yeehawed, and that meant the ranch was in sight.

Everyone who'd been left behind would be waiting for them, to help funnel the cattle into appropriate pastures where they'd be able to get to them easier come Market Day next month. The cows would continue to get fat closer to the epicenter, and the hills and wild lands of the ranch would regrow for next season's herd.

Beau rode a pretty brown horse named Gingersnap, and she'd done a good job for him on this roundup. So he leaned over and patted her neck. "Almost back, Gingy." He could admit he was ready to be done smelling like horses and cattle, eating out of a can, and plenty of other things, but what he wanted the most was to see Charlotte.

She'd had the cabin to herself for the past five nights, and half of him worried that she'd have replaced the furniture and changed all the curtains, paint colors, and dish towels to a shade of pastel he'd never be able to eradicate.

He smiled just thinking about the pinks and purples...and Charlotte. He scrubbed his hand down his beard, getting plenty of dust and shards of alfalfa that kicked up into the air. Everything itched, and his mood soured slightly that he still sat in the saddle.

He coached himself through it, because Beau had been through plenty of roundups and cattle drives. No sense in getting all worked up over it. He coughed and lifted his bandana up to cover his mouth.

Cheering met them as they continued to bring in the herd. He couldn't see individual faces from where he rode, but plenty of people waved bandanas and flags as they yelled about their triumphant return. He and Gingerbread continued to do their job, and when every last cow had been sorted and put in a pasture, Beau headed for the stables.

It would be busy, as he wasn't the only man eager to be out of the sun and in the shower. His head ached, but he kept it down and got Gingy cleaned up and fed and watered, put away comfortably in her stall, and started back toward the cabin.

Charlotte led a horse toward him, a huge smile on her face. "You're back."

His own smile filled his whole face. "Wow, you are the only person I want to see right now." He stifled a cough and took her effortlessly into his arms. He didn't care who saw them, as everyone on the ranch knew they were dating.

He kissed her slowly, passionately, and stepped back as the horse beside them huffed. "Oh, you're ready for a nap, Courtside?" He chuckled as he patted the horse. "You're putting him away? Where's Jerry?"

"He wasn't feeling well," Charlotte said. "Bad headache."

"Mine's not feeling great either," Beau said. "But I'll shower and take some meds, and we'll head to the feast, okay?"

"Sure, yeah." She picked up the lead rope again. "I'm just helping anyone who needs it."

"Yeah, you're making sure your stable gets put back together how you want it."

Charlotte only grinned at him and continued down the aisle. Beau chuckled to himself and went on home, the touch of hot water on his skin the most welcome thing he'd experienced that week.

He tilted his face back into it and let it flow through his hair, cleansing him. "It's good to be home," he murmured into the water. And alone. Beau felt like he was a social creature, but he also liked his alone-time at home.

The dinner that night would be filled with people—everyone from the ranch, from Courage Reins, and from Bowman's Breeds—and since his birthday was so close, he suspected Kelly would have cake there.

She usually did, as the roundup sometimes went over his birthday. It had become part of the tradition here at Three

Rivers, and Beau always felt so loved when so many voices sang *Happy Birthday* to him.

His momma would call tomorrow, as would his sisters, and Beau did enjoy celebrating with them, even from afar. He'd had a few Septembers alone, and he'd really been looking forward to celebrating with Charlotte.

When he was dressed again, he headed out to the kitchen, lamenting the fact that he had to put boots on again to leave the cabin.

"Happy birthday, baby."

Beau came to a stop and looked over to Charlotte. She stood on the other side of the kitchen island, and several candles burned atop a birthday cake sitting between them. He chuckled and looked from the blue frosting to her. "I'm older than nine."

"Yeah, forty," she teased. She nodded slightly to the cake. "Make a wish and blow them out."

"My birthday is tomorrow."

"I'm aware. We both took the afternoon off so we could go take a nap in the movie theater before dinner." She grinned at him.

Beau smiled on back. They'd operate on a holiday schedule for the next couple of days as men and horses rested up, and it hadn't been hard to get the afternoon off. "I thought we'd have cake then."

"I wanted to celebrate with you before the whole ranch did." She came toward him and ran her hands up his chest. A shiver moved through his bloodstream, and he told himself it was because he hadn't felt the cool kiss of air conditioning in a while.

"Celebrate, huh?"

"I have never lived alone," she whispered, running the tip of her nose along his jawline.

"You don't live alone now."

"But I did for the past few nights." She pulled back and tucked herself into his arms. Beau had never come back from the roundup to a woman like this, and he could get very used to it. This place of comfort, where he could tell her how much he'd yearned to be here, and all about the stars he'd laid awake watching one night, and how Pepper had kept him awake with his snoring another night.

"And I didn't like it," Charlotte added.

"Sorry I took both dogs."

"They need baths."

"Tomorrow," he said. "How are the donkeys?"

"I think they missed you more than I did."

"Is that so?" He pulled back and looked at her. "Well, I didn't miss them more than I missed you." He kissed her then, keeping it slow and steady and oh-so-meaningful. And the best part was he didn't have to stop when a fussy horse wanted to get back to his stable.

"We'll be late to the party."

"Yeah, I know." Beau kept kissing her, not a care in the world as he fell further and further in love with his cabinmate.

* * *

The following afternoon, Beau woke to Charlotte giggling. "Wake up, cowboy." Darkness surrounded them, and he opened his eyes to the scrolling credits of the movie he'd chosen for his birthday. Not even a spy action movie could keep him awake.

"Sorry." He turned his head to look at her, a smile on his face. "I didn't mean to fall asleep."

"It's your birthday," she said, smiling prettily back at him. "You should get to do what you want."

"Well, we have to go to the feed store before dinner, and I don't want to do that."

"Why'd you say you would then?"

"Because it's a ninety-minute round-trip we were already making." He sighed and sat up. A groan came from his mouth, and he scrubbed both hands down his face, trying to get himself to wake up more fully.

Beside him, Charlotte picked up their half-eaten popcorn bucket and piled in her soda cup. He got to his feet and took the trash from her, and they left the theater.

At the feed store, he said, "I'll just run in and grab the stuff from the back."

But Charlotte had unbuckled her seatbelt and was turning toward the passenger door as if she'd get out too. "Sure, okay," she said. "I'm going to run next door and get a couple more of those shower steamers." She flashed him a smile, but Beau simply sat in the driver's seat.

When he didn't get out, she leaned back in. "Oh, don't wear such a sour face. You liked the seabreeze one."

"Okay, but don't get that weird chamomile one or whatever."

"It was matcha and bergamot." She grinned at him and laced her purse over her shoulder.

"It was gross," he called after her as she slammed the door. He didn't shower in her bathroom, but her steamers filled the whole cabin with a certain smell.

He got out of the truck and waved to her giggling form as she headed across the parking lot toward the beauty store that sold her beloved shower steamers. Beau pushed his way into the feed store and headed straight for the back pick-up counter. He just needed a couple of boxes of the fly control spray for the cattle now that they were back from the range.

Squire had called it in already, and all Beau had to do was give his name and pick up the products. A couple of cowboys waited at the pick-up counter ahead of him, but they had plenty of people working. Beau wouldn't have any problem getting the fly spray before Charlotte managed to browse through all of her shower steamer scents.

He sidled up behind the cowboy in front of him, something very familiar about him. The man looked at something on his phone, and when he noticed or felt Beau's presence, he looked at him.

Recognition sparked, and Beau laughed. "Mason."

Charlotte's brother turned as he laughed. "Howdy, Beau." They shook hands and did a quick cowboy-hug before separating again. "What brings you to town?"

"Just getting the fly control spray for the cattle. We got 'em all back in."

Mason nodded, his dark eyes glinting with joy. "That's great." He nodded to his phone. "My cowboys should be back within the hour with our herd."

"You didn't go?"

Mason shook his head, his attention back on his phone. "I sent my foreman and my cowboys." He looked up. "Does your owner go on the roundup?"

"Yeah," Beau said, a little surprised Mason hadn't gone to fetch his own cattle. "He's our vet, so yeah, he goes."

Mason nodded. "How's Char?"

"Good," Beau said quickly. Maybe a little too quickly. "We're out—it's my birthday."

His best friend's face burst into a grin. "Oh, that's right. Happy birthday, brother." He hugged him again. The line inched forward and they went with it, now standing more side-by-side.

Mason still had a couple of people in front of him, both being helped by people behind the counter. "She's doing okay? No fainting spells?"

"She's great," Beau said. "One of the best people I've seen work with horses."

"Right," Mason said. "But she's okay?"

"I've been keepin' an eye on her," Beau said. "Like you asked." He gave his friend a side-eyed look. He hadn't really been watching for slips in Charlotte's health for a while now. He trusted her to tell him when she wasn't feeling well, and she did.

"She just doesn't say much to us," Mason said. "She's an expert at keeping secrets."

Beau hadn't known that to be true. Charlotte did like to hold things close to the vest until she was ready to talk about them. It didn't mean she was secretive.

"She's had a couple of incidents," Beau said. "I didn't think—"

"A couple of incidents?"

Beau turned around to find Charlotte standing there, her purse slung over her shoulder. "You're reporting about me to my brother?" She threw a furious look at Mason and then fixed those blazing hot, angry eyes on Beau.

"It's not like that," he said.

She held up one hand. "They were out of steamers." She spun on her heel and marched away from him, leaving Beau torn about going after her and waiting for his fly control spray.

Go!

He wasn't sure who spoke, but he took it as a command from God, and Beau didn't even offer an explanation to Mason. He simply ran after Charlotte, calling, "Little bird, wait."

Chapter Sixteen

"Little bird." She scoffed as she stormed out of the feed store. Beau would only be a moment behind her, but she didn't care. She wasn't his little bird—at least not one he held gently in his hands and cherished.

He viewed her as something broken and helpless. Something he had to cage behind closed fingers and keep close, because she couldn't take care of herself.

"Charlotte," he said as he spilled out of the store.

"Go get your stuff," she said over her shoulder. She yanked open the passenger door of his truck and glared at him, daring him to come closer. He seemed to sense the danger, because he stopped on the sidewalk. "I'll just sit here and wait. That's what you wanted, right?"

"Charlotte, of course not."

She vaulted into the truck and slammed the door, refusing to look at him again. Petty, perhaps. Childish, for sure.

But she did *not* need the mighty Beau Peterson to protect her. Or spy on her and send reports to Mason. She blinked, and everything in her life turned red. Charlotte took a deep breath and prayed, "Lord, help me to calm down."

Her heartbeat raced, and then it suddenly stopped. Her head felt too heavy and then too light, and she looked over to Beau. He stood on the curb, watching her with a frown etched in all the lines on his face.

Charlotte's throat closed, and she couldn't get a breath to go into her lungs. Whiteness started to crowd in around the edges of her vision. She pressed her first and second fingers together and started to lift her hand, but Beau was already moving toward her.

A moment later, before she'd completed the nonverbal sign that she needed help, he pulled open the passenger door and said, "Hey, hey, hey."

She slumped into him as she started to lose consciousness, and she hated her heart with everything inside her. Why did it have to betray her like this? She'd just wanted someone to see her for who she was—a strong woman. A good horse trainer. A valuable partner in life.

Not her faulty heart.

"I got you, little bird," Beau whispered. "It's okay. You just got mad at me over something silly, but your heartbeat will calm down, and I'll be right here."

Charlotte hadn't passed out, but her eyes had closed. She could still hear him, and the warmth of his body next to hers brought her comfort and a sense of safety.

"When you wake up, you'll see that I didn't mean anything

by what I said to Mason." He sighed and stroked her hair off her forehead. "Dear God, how do I help her understand? It was nothing. A throwaway conversation while we waited in line."

He sounded absolutely agonized, and Charlotte didn't want him to hurt.

"I can't lose her," he whispered. "Okay, Charlotte? I'm not going anywhere, because I can't lose you."

She took one calming breath and started to feel more like herself. Then another. "I'm awake," she whispered, and she pushed against his chest to sit up straight. She felt too hot, sitting in the truck without the air conditioning running.

Charlotte looked over to Beau, standing there framed in the doorway of the truck. "I—"

"Just let me apologize," he said. "It was nothing. Mason just asked me how you were. I said you were fine, and he pressed me. So I said you'd had a couple of incidents, but what I was going to say after that, before you interrupted, was that it was nothing you couldn't handle. That you work hard and got a headache one day, and you were doing great. Amazing. Phenomenal."

His chest heaved, and Charlotte did find him absolutely adorable. "I believe you."

"I—what?"

"Maybe I got mad too fast." She shrugged one shoulder and looked out the windshield. "And then I ran away, and I wasn't breathing, and—" She switched her gaze to his. "I do not need you to protect me."

"Of course you don't," he said. "But Charlotte, is it such a bad thing that I want to? Heck, I'd love it if someone protected me. Someone who makes me birthday cakes that we can enjoy away from the cowboy crowds, and thinks of me when she's shopping for shower steamers, and always thinks of how she can help others around the ranch."

He backed up. "I'll start the truck." He cleared his throat as he went around the hood. Behind the wheel, he started the truck and looked over to her. "I'll be right back. You're welcome to come in. We can go shopping anywhere else you want. Maybe head over to the outdoor mall to a different bath store."

Charlotte looked over to him, and she just wanted her slow, sensual afternoon and evening with him. "I'm sorry I got mad so fast."

"It's okay," Beau said. "I know why you did." He gave her a fast flash of a smile and then got out of the truck and headed back inside.

Mason happened to be coming out at the same time, and the two of them stopped to talk to one another for a few seconds. Nothing too long, and neither of them looked at her when the conversation finished.

Beau continued inside; Mason turned to his right and headed to his truck. Charlotte sighed and leaned her head back against the rest, a prayer of her own starting to stream through her mind.

Lord, I don't want to lose Beau either.

She sighed. "I thought I'd grown a little bit." As she sat there and waited, she really felt like she had. She didn't rely on anyone anymore. No, she hadn't liked sleeping in the cabin alone while Beau was out on the roundup, but she'd still had a few horses to take care of in his absence.

She could do her job. Not only that, but she was really good at it. "I love it," she whispered to the blowing AC. She did love her job, and she wanted to keep it for as long as possible.

Beau came outside, two small cases in his arms. "Do you love him?"

Charlotte wasn't sure, because she'd never been in love before. She knew she didn't want to lose him, and after he'd put the boxes in the back, he got behind the wheel to her saying, "I don't want to lose you either."

She reached out, relieved and glad when Beau immediately stretched forth his hand too. He captured hers in his, once again giving her a beautiful sense of safety. "You heard that, huh?"

She nodded at him. "Can we go to dinner now?"

"You don't want to try to find a shower steamer?"

Charlotte shook her head now, everything feeling soft. "I just want to spend time with you—and get some onion rings."

Beau smiled at her, really turning on his mega-watt grin. The one he used when he was flirting, and the one he used when he truly felt joy and happiness.

"I'll get you whatever you want to eat, my little bird."

"Thank you, Beau," she said. Their eyes met, and Beau leaned toward her. She did the same, meeting him for a sweet kiss over the console. His hand slid up her neck, lighting little fires in every cell he touched.

"You don't say my name very often," he whispered against

her lips before kissing her again. He pulled back again. "I like it."

She ducked her head and settled back into her own seat. Beau buckled his seatbelt, and she copied him, so they could go to dinner for his birthday. She didn't want to be upset with him, especially not on the day he was turning forty.

"Did you talk to your mom this morning?"

He shook his head. "She hasn't called yet."

"So probably during dinner."

He backed out of the parking stall. "I can talk to her and Dolly and Amy tomorrow."

Charlotte looked over to him as he drove. "Do you miss your daddy?"

"Yeah." He nodded, his face hard and stoic. "Yep. A lot today."

"I'm sorry, cowboy." She took his hand in hers and squeezed. "I'm glad I get to be here on your birthday."

"I've had a lot of birthdays by myself lately," he said. "So I'm real glad you're here too." He lifted her hand to his mouth and kissed the back of it. The streets went by as he navigated them to the restaurant he'd chosen for his birthday dinner.

Charlotte's thoughts needled at her, and she finally turned toward him again. "Beau, do you think I've changed since coming to the ranch?"

"Yeah," he said easily. "Of course you have."

"How?"

"You want me to tell you how you've changed?"

She sighed, irritated with herself. "I just got so mad so fast in there, and I hate that I did. I feel like I've been working on that, and I don't know. Now I feel like I haven't made any progress at all."

"Everyone gets mad sometimes," he said.

"Do they? What would it take for you to go from zero to sixty and lose your temper?"

"Reckless cowboys," he said. Then he chuckled and shook his head. "Which is funny, because I'm pretty sure that was how I was viewed at one point."

"You and Ben." She grinned at him.

He pulled into Thompson House Kitchen & Bar, where they were eating that night. "Yeah." He chuckled. "Me and Ben."

"But you grew up."

"That I did." He found a parking spot and looked at her. "All the way to forty. I feel so old."

Charlotte giggled, but she secretly liked that he was older than her. He dropped from the truck and came around to get her door.

Beau opened her door and took her hand in his as she slid out. "Little bird?"

"Yeah?"

He led her toward the entrance. "Do you want kids?"

Charlotte hadn't been expecting the question, and a bolt of surprise shot through her. Her next step stumbled, and to Beau's credit, he didn't slow down or ask her if she was okay. He simply held her hand as she righted herself and waited.

"I've never really thought about it," she said honestly.

Inside the restaurant, music played and people talked, and it was a loud atmosphere.

Beau had a reservation, and they got shown to a quieter table against the window. He took his menu, and Charlotte took hers, but instead of looking at it, she said, "I'd like kids."

He looked up. "Yeah?"

"Do you want kids?"

"I have for a while now, yeah," he said. "I just see my friends and their families, and it's become this, this...I don't know, this need inside of me."

She nodded. "Now that I'm at Three Rivers, I can see that I can live by myself. I can date and find someone to love, and maybe just now, I started to see a future with kids."

"Interesting," he said as he went back to his menu.

Charlotte found it interesting too, and she smiled to herself as she hid behind the menu too. *I really have changed*, she thought. And the man across from her had played a vital role in all of that.

She chanced a peek at Beau, and she felt something she'd never felt before. Her heart beat in a way she'd never experienced before, and she couldn't give it any other name but....

Love.

Just as quickly as that feeling had come and she'd classified it, an overwhelming sense of fear flooded her. She pulled in a tight breath, which drew Beau's attention. He raised his eyebrows, but she just shook her head.

And because he was so good and so kind, he went back to the menu without challenging her further. She'd talk about this when she could, and that moment was not right now, on her cowboy boyfriend's birthday.

No, she wasn't going to live in fear and ask him a bunch of questions tonight. She just wanted to be with him and share a good experience with him for his birthday. So that was exactly what she was going to do.

Chapter Seventeen

Beau brushed his teeth, his only thought of how amazing this birthday had been. And to think, six months ago, he'd been dreading it. Of course, six months ago, he hadn't met Charlotte yet, and his current Stable Manager had just announced that he'd be leaving soon.

He definitely had a lot to be grateful for, and when he finished brushing, he moved to his bedside and dropped to his knees. "Heavenly Father."

His mind went on the fritz then, because he had so many beautiful things in his life right now. He couldn't possibly thank God for all of them. Beau drew a breath and attempted to focus.

"Thank you for my momma," he started. "I miss her, Lord, and I know I need to get her and Amy up here for a visit."

The problem was he much preferred his sister Dolly to his sister Amy, and he'd have to pay for the trip, as his family didn't have much money.

"Thank you for this ranch," he said, something he thanked the Lord for every single night. He'd found a true brotherhood here. A family. People to love and care about who loved and cared about him too. "If there's something I should be doing to help anyone here, please open my eyes and my mind to them. Inspire me to know how to help them."

Beau had once heard Pete pray like this, and it had touched his heart so deeply, he'd taken it into his own prayers.

"Thank you for forty years on this planet," he whispered. "And for a great day with Charlotte."

Ah, Charlotte.

"Thank you for Charlotte." Beau paused and let his feelings paint through him. "I'm falling in love with her, and I'm terrified."

He'd felt things shift between them, even though she'd apologized for getting mad so fast. Of course he'd accepted the apology, because it felt genuine and real. But she'd stuffed something away, and Beau had let her.

He could revert to his flirty, fun self, so he wouldn't fall further. He could put distance between them while laughing with her and kissing her; he'd done it in other relationships where he wasn't as into the woman as she was him. Or when he'd started to fall and he could tell his girlfriend didn't like him as much as he did her.

But with Charlotte, she didn't know how to be inauthentic. "Mason said she keeps secrets," he said. "Lord, if she's keeping something from me, bless me to know. Bless me to know what to do when it comes to her."

Pull back to spare his heart? Or finally let himself fall all the way in love, even if it shattered everything inside him?

He stayed on his knees, listening, but he didn't get any answers right then. So he said, "Thank you for my life, Lord. Thank you for giving Your life to make it possible for me to repent and be saved. Amen."

Beau got to his feet, his forty-year-old knees a little too old to stay down that long. He groaned as he got into bed and reached to switch off his lamp. "It was a really great day," he whispered, and then he fell asleep, knowing he had a full day of work ahead of him tomorrow.

But he didn't dream of horses and cows and fly spray. He didn't see himself eating with other cowboys and coming home alone.

He saw himself alongside Charlotte, the two of them riding horses out to an overnight cabin, where they ate a picnic lunch beside a stream, the blue Texas sky overhead, and everything perfect between them.

Hardly any of Beau's dreams had ever come true, but he had never felt this good about a relationship before. He clung to that with all he had, and the dream stayed with him even after he woke.

* * *

By evening, Beau was only dreaming of a hot meal and a soft bed. Anything that could go wrong that day, had gone wrong. The truck that brought their fertilizer and small animal feed had broken down, and Beau had sent several cowboys to help get their items off the truck as it sat on the side of the highway.

That put them behind on getting the cattle checked for insect bites, hoof injuries, and any number of other health problems. They had less than a month until Market Day, and Beau's whole job depended on having their cattle ready to sell for top dollar.

Not only that, but Mother Nature had decided to bake the Panhandle, and he hadn't been this hot since mid-July. And God was playing some horrible trick on him by making his throat itch and burn all day long.

He absolutely could not get sick, so he'd texted his mother for her home remedies, and he fully planned to drink a gallon of tea with honey when he got home.

When he finally got back to the cabin for the night, he expected to see Charlotte—whom he hadn't seen all day—in the living room. Maybe on her phone, with the TV playing something so she didn't have to be alone. She'd told him that was what she'd done while he was gone on the roundup—play the TV and pretend those people were in the room with her.

Maybe she'd be in the kitchen, scrambling eggs or heating up something from the freezer they could both eat.

He didn't expect the cabin to be sitting in evening shadows, silent and empty. He hadn't come home to this in a while, and he did not like it. "Charlotte?" he called as he hung his hat on the hook next to the front door. His head pounded, but he ignored it for the moment.

Pepper and Ruby came laboring inside, because they'd all had a very long day. Sunrise to sunset, and while Beau didn't usually mind it, today, he did. Charlotte didn't answer, and Beau got busy feeding and watering the dogs.

He normally showered before dinner, but his hollow stomach shouted at him to eat first. He made himself a ham and cheese sandwich, wondering if Charlotte was still at work or not. He'd been diverting people all day, and she did have a lot to do to care for the horses that had been out on the roundup for a week.

He set a tea kettle to warm for his mother's home remedy, and he threw back some painkillers that actually hurt his throat as he swallowed them.

As he finished his sandwich, he went down the hall to his bedroom. Her door sat closed, which wasn't that unusual. He left his open during the day, but she rarely did. He'd not been inside the bedroom since he'd cared for her when she'd had her headache, and he gave the door a cursory glance and continued into his bedroom.

He closed and locked the door behind him and sent her a quick text. *I'm home and getting in the shower. Where are you? Did you get dinner?*

Before he'd stripped out of his dirty clothes, she answered with, *I'm home, showered, and I've eaten. My mom called, and I'm talking to her in my bedroom.*

Oh, great, he said. Not sure what else to say, he left his phone on the nightstand and went to shower.

The next day, a loft in one of Pete's barns broke, and Beau had sent several cowboys to help rebuild it on the fly. An ambulance had been called for the two cowboys who'd fallen two stories with the hay and rotted flooring.

He didn't get home until dusk that evening too, and once again, he walked into a semi-dark, silent, empty cabin. "Charlotte?" he called again, feeling eerily like he'd entered another dimension where he was living the same day over and over again, but with different calamities during the day.

But at night, he had to go home alone. Hungry. Too hot. And with a headache and that pesky sore throat. His mother claimed more vitamins and zinc supplements would ward off the impending sickness, and Beau happened to have the things she claimed would save him.

He heard Charlotte's shower running as he passed the mouth of the hall, and he fed and watered the dogs, made himself a sandwich, drank the orange-flavored vitamins with a side of zinc, and texted his cabinmate from the safety of his locked bedroom.

Been a long day, she said. *I'm going to finish some notes for the horses and go to bed early.*

Beau did the same. He woke up the next morning and did his Sunrise Cowboy live-stream with hardly a voice. His head hurt this morning, when it usually didn't start to ache until lunchtime. He coughed as he said, "Until tomorrow's sunrise, have a good one, doing good things and living good lives."

He spent the morning in his air-conditioned office, trying to put together a schedule for the upcoming harvest. They were a couple of days late getting started, and Beau sent men to town to pick up the equipment they needed.

That put them down a few hands on the ranch, and that forced Beau out of the admin building and into the blazing heatwave to work alongside his men. After all, animals had to be tended to, as did seemingly everything else on this ranch.

When he and the dogs walked into a dark, silent, empty cabin for the third night in a row, Beau realized there was a problem. Not one on the ranch. Not one a few texts could fix. Not one he could send a couple of cowhands to help with.

But a problem between him and Charlotte.

He didn't know how to fix phantom problems. Give him a schedule and a pile of men, and he'd figure it out. He knew how to organize a harvest with dozens of people, machines, and fields.

But a woman who'd gone silent on him? Whom he lived with?

Beau only knew how to do one thing in a situation like this: Flirt.

So he pulled out his phone and sent Charlotte a message.

Chapter Eighteen

Charlotte knew the moment Beau walked into the cabin. Not from hearing the door or the dogs or even him. His personality, the very essence of him, radiated with such power and charisma, she simply knew.

She looked up from her laptop, which she'd put on the bed in front of her, wondering what she should do. She still wasn't entirely sure how she felt about Beau, and she'd told herself after his amazing birthday, with such a great dinner and even better kissing, that she'd take some time to figure things out.

Her work around the ranch had exploded, as cowboys she relied on to help her with the horses had been called in different directions this week. Still, she managed to make it home before Beau, and she'd wolf down something for dinner or bring it into her room, shower as fast as possible, and sequester herself behind the closed bedroom door.

Beau had texted her both nights, and her phone chimed as she reached for it to message him first.

Did you move out? I feel like I'm living alone again, and I'm not sure I like it. He'd added a laughing emoji, but nothing inside Charlotte felt like laughing.

She could respond via text the way she had the other evenings. Her computer played streaming TV and videos just fine, and she'd used headphones so Beau wouldn't know she hadn't gone straight to bed when she'd claimed to be so tired.

And she *was* tired. That hadn't been a lie.

But mostly tired from her confusing thoughts and feelings.

Instead of hiding behind her phone, she got up and left the bedroom. It only took her a few steps to get down the hall, where she found Beau filling a bowl with water for Pepper and Ruby. "I didn't move out," she said.

He jerked, obviously startled, and water sloshed out of the bowl. "Charlotte," he said in a gaspy voice. "You scared me."

She gave him a quick smile he didn't really receive, as focused on the water bowl as he was. "Sorry."

"Good thing I don't have vasovagal syncope, or I'd have passed out." He bent to put the bowl on the floor, and when he rose, he wore a bright smile that didn't fit the mood between them.

Ah, he'd gone into Public Relations mode. The Beau he wanted everyone to see and love, not the man she'd been steadily falling for.

"Did you eat?"

"Yes," she said.

He opened the fridge and promptly closed it again. "We don't have anything good."

"I can go to the grocery store."

"Right now?"

"I mean—"

He faced her, something hard etched onto his face. "I don't want you to go. I don't want to be here alone."

Charlotte wasn't sure how to respond. It felt like someone had blown sand in her face, and she couldn't see which way to go.

"I'm going to make a sandwich and take a shower," he said as he came around the island between them. "Can you not disappear, please?" He grinned at her and wrapped his arms around her. She could admit it felt warm and wonderful to be held by him.

So maybe she did love him. Or at least was falling in that direction.

And would that be so bad?

He nuzzled her neck and said, "Mm, you smell fruity and fun." He lifted his head. "Give me twenty minutes, and I don't care if we don't talk. I just don't want to sit at my—*our*—dark, silent cabin alone for one more night."

She nodded, her voice balled up somewhere in her throat. Beau never seemed to have that problem, as his mouth always said what it wanted to. He eased away from her and went about making his sandwich, using the last of the ham and cheese. They really would have to get to the grocery store soon.

"We're working with Marlin tomorrow, right?" he asked as he capped his sandwich with the second piece of bread.

"Yes," she said.

"Then we can talk horses tonight, if you want." He raised

his eyebrows, those gorgeous eyes almost too pretty for her to look into for more than a moment.

"That would be great."

He gave her that dazzling, flirty smile and headed down the hall to his bedroom. If they could talk about the horses tonight, then Charlotte wouldn't have to tell him why she'd retreated a little bit.

Maybe she could just make a comeback and never have to say anything about it at all. She scoffed as she moved toward the back door, where Pepper and Ruby ate their dinner with crunches and slurps.

She sank onto the floor there and absently stroked Ruby's pretty fur. "He's going to make me talk, isn't he?"

The collie didn't answer her. In fact, Ruby rarely used her voice. That was more Pepper's style, and Charlotte simply wanted to escape the four walls of the cabin. The walls that she'd put up around herself needed to come down too, but she wasn't quite sure how to do it.

"If you don't," she whispered to herself. "You'll lose Beau."

And that struck like a bolt of lightning right into the fleshy part of her heart. She didn't want to lose Beau. Not to her own stubbornness, her own inability to rely on someone who wanted to take care of her.

"You don't keep secrets," she told herself. "You've changed." She leaned her head back and looked up to the loft, where Beau kept his live-streaming supplies: tripod, ring light, extra cords. "I'm different, right, Lord? I feel so different."

She'd been praying for a way to talk to Beau, for a way to

know how she felt about him. Precisely know. No answers had come.

But as she sat on the kitchen floor while the dogs finished their dinner, she knew one thing. She had to talk to Mason before she could take the next step with Beau.

"Mason?" she wondered. Why would she need to talk to him?

She wasn't sure, but she seized onto the feeling, because it felt very much like God telling her what to do, and she didn't want to ignore that.

Charlotte also didn't want to talk to Mason. At all. Not even a little bit.

But she got to her feet and opened the back door. She and the dogs went outside, where they settled in the shade of the tree where she'd found the canines on moving day, and she tapped to call her brother.

Mason always had his phone with him, she wasn't surprised when he said, "Heya, Char," only a moment later.

Something stormed inside her, muting her voice. Something she recognized as...angry. She wasn't sure she'd ever been truly angry at Mason before. He'd done so much for her over the years. Provided her way of life, took care of her, protected her.

Shielded her. Talked down to her. Criticized her. Caged her.

Maybe not all true, but she let the feelings romp through her however they wanted.

"Charlotte, are you hurt? Are you there? Do you need help?"

She took a breath, and said, "Just the fact that you think I'm hurt and need help says so much."

"It says what?" he fired back. "You didn't answer when I answered. *You* called *me*."

She didn't want to fight with him, and all that negativity simply streamed out of her. Someone had definitely just helped her, because she hadn't been able to let go of so much until that very moment.

Yes, I am with you.

Buoyed by the strength of Jesus, she took another breath. "I'm okay," she said in a much softer voice. "Mason, how did you know you loved Felicity and wanted to be with her?"

"I—" he cut off, clearly not expecting this radical change in Charlotte's demeanor. She could go from hot to cold and back at any moment, and she'd been working on her temper. She really had been.

And she really wanted Mason to know that, to see it, to understand that she was capable of taking care of herself.

"Thank you for all you did for me," she said next, the words just there. The sweetest feeling of forgiveness ran through her. "I've been blaming you for some things that might not be entirely fair, but it really hurt when you told Beau I was an expert at keeping secrets."

"Charlotte," Mason said just as quietly. "I know I overstep with you sometimes. I'm sorry about that."

She leaned her head back against the trunk of the tree behind her. "You and Felicity and the kids have been so good to me. I love it here at Three Rivers so much." She pressed her eyes closed. "And I really like Beau, Mace. I *really* like him."

"I know you do." His tone carried a hint of displeasure, and Charlotte wanted to root it out and watch it die.

"Why does that upset you?"

"It's just...you haven't dated a lot, Char. Just because he's the first man who comes along and sweeps you off your feet doesn't mean it's a forever love."

"Is there a number of men I need to date before that will happen?"

"No, of course not."

"Then why not him?"

"It's just—he's—honestly, I'm surprised you guys get along as well as you do. He just doesn't seem like your type."

"What would be my type?"

"Charlotte."

"No, I'm serious, Mace. We had *such* a great time on his birthday, and I think I'm falling in love with him. But I've never been in love before, and I'm...."

Scared. Confused. Worried.

Any number of words could fill that pause, and thankfully, Mason didn't run his mouth and try to do it.

"Trying to make sense of things," she said. "I'm trying to make sense of things."

"Just take it," Mason said, and Charlotte wasn't sure what was happening. Then Felicity came on the line with, "You think you're in love with him?"

"I don't know," she said with a sigh. "How do you know?"

"Okay, honey, listen to me." Felicity had her Mom-Boss voice turned on, and Charlotte actually smiled. "Love is not something you can write on your clipboard, Charlotte. It's not something you analyze or find a rational pathway through. There are no checklists or numbers of men you need to go out with."

Her smile widened, because surely Felicity had just shot a death glare in Mason's direction.

"It's something you feel," Felicity said. "You have to allow yourself to *feel* it. It just comes, and when it does, Char, it's so beautiful and wonderful. And you'll just...know."

"What if I'm past feeling?" Charlotte asked. "You know how I am, Felicity. I'm so harsh sometimes." Tears filled her eyes. "What if it's there, and I just can't feel it?"

"Being stubborn and harsh is not the same as being a sociopath."

Charlotte burst out laughing, her tears still stuck in the corners of her eyes, but everything so much happier now. "A sociopath."

Felicity giggled with her, then sobered. "Seriously, Charlotte. Just let yourself go. Then you'll know."

"Thank you, Felicity," she whispered.

"Do you want to talk to Mason again?"

Charlotte considered it for a moment, really trying to listen to that voice that sometimes entered her head. It didn't come. "No," she said. "I think I'm good. I love you guys. Kiss the kids for me, and tell them I'm going to come visit really soon."

"We all miss you terribly," Felicity said. "I'm putting you on speaker. Kids, it's Charlotte. Tell her you love her!"

Yells and shouts of adoration came through the line, and Charlotte let herself feel those. They sank right into her soul, and she knew she was so loved.

Now, she just had to figure out how to let herself feel her own feelings and decide if they were love or not. She ended the call and opened her eyes, the gentle breeze only slightly cooling the evening heat.

"There you are," Beau said a few minutes later. "I thought you'd run off."

She got to her feet, because she knew he didn't want to sit outside and bake. She didn't really want to either. She approached Beau, who grinned at her in that impish cowboy way he had. "Guess what I found in the freezer?"

Charlotte climbed the steps to join him on the back deck. "What?"

He held up a gallon-sized Ziplock bag. "Cookie dough. Come on, we're bingeing on oatmeal chocolate chip tonight."

She laughed as she followed him inside, and then she took over the cookie prep. "You're sick," she said. "Go lie down and I'll bring in the treats."

He did what she said, and she recognized that they'd perhaps put a bandage over the wounds between them. It might hold for a little while longer, but it might just get ripped off and cause more bleeding too.

But Charlotte didn't have the words that would stitch everything up neatly and nicely, so she used a knife to cut cubes out of the frozen cookie dough, and when the first batch had baked, she took a plate over to the couch where Beau...had fallen asleep.

He was cowboy perfect when he didn't carry the weight of the ranch on his face. So handsome, and while those eyes she loved couldn't be seen, the pure goodness of him made up for it.

Her feelings expanded, and while her first instinct was to pull back, harness the power of them, she forced herself to let them go. They didn't go far, and she brushed his hair off his forehead with, "Cookies are done, cowboy."

Beau didn't stir, which testified of how tired and sick he truly was. So Charlotte leaned down and barely touched her lips to his skin, getting plenty of sizzle and spark from that simple act.

And she knew—on some level, she loved this man, and now she just needed to figure out how to tell him.

Chapter Nineteen

"You're being really stubborn," Beau called down to Charlotte, which earned him a glare. He bent his arm and coughed into his elbow. He'd been home from the roundup for a week now, and he'd been fighting a sore throat every morning since.

He'd faithfully done all of his mother's home remedies. Tea with honey. Extra doses of vitamins, taken with a couple of zinc pills. All of them—and none of them had worked.

Beau had to face facts: He was sick.

Charlotte was working with a horse named Marlin, and both of them looked past quitting time. He'd told her as much, as they were the only two gathered around the ring today. She'd ignored him, her strong personality shining through in that moment.

Since his birthday, she'd definitely re-erected some of the walls she'd come to the ranch with, but Beau didn't know how to kick them back down. The truth was, he'd reverted back to the flirtatious cowboy he'd been in his twenties and early thirties too.

He wasn't sure why they'd both taken a step backward, other than it made life in the cabin easier.

When Marlin still wouldn't go right, Beau whistled down to her. "Charlotte, I'm calling it. He's exhausted, and so am I."

"Fine." She moved toward the horse while he got down from the fence. He opened the gate for her to lead the equine through, and she wouldn't look at him as she walked by.

"You can't be mad at me over this," he said. "Bribe him with some of your strawberry candies or something."

She swung the horse around to face him. "Candy only works when you're getting to know a horse."

"Oh, it does not." Beau swung the gate closed and faced her too. "It works when you want them to stop biting at their bandages, and when you want them to like you, and when you're overworking them."

"Beau."

"You're not the only person who's ever worked with a horse before, you know." The moment he said it, he regretted it. He started to cough before he could apologize, and he held up one hand while he coughed into the other.

"Sorry," he said. "I'm sorry. I'm just exhausted and sick. I didn't mean it. I don't mean to snap at you, I swear." He took a couple of steps toward her and took the rope from her. He held it as he pulled her into his chest. "There's something going on between us, and I'm not sure what it is, but I don't like it."

Charlotte didn't say anything, and Beau let her go. "We haven't been out all week. You disappear into your room at night. Can we...I'm going to make breakfast for dinner tonight. For us. Okay?"

They didn't have everything he wanted to make, but he could send a text out to his friends and get the extra eggs and sausage he needed. Easy.

Why wasn't falling in love as easy? Why did it have to be so hard?

Why hadn't Charlotte said *okay* yet?

Beau handed her the rope and said, "I actually really like how stubborn you are with the horses."

She softened, maybe for the first time this week. "Okay."

"Things have been different, right?"

"They've been a little different."

"Charlotte," Kenny called, and they both turned toward the other cowboy. "Beau! We've got horses out at Brynn's, and we need all available men in the saddle."

Of course they did.

This week, he thought.

His head pounded, and Beau just wanted to go home and get something ice-cold to drink to soothe the fire in his throat. "Did it go out on text?"

"She's sending it now." Kenny took the rope from Charlotte. "I'll put him away and start saddling for others."

"I'll go with you." The two of them left, and Beau couldn't just stand there. Brynn's horses weren't all trained, and even those that were possessed an almost wild spirit, as she trained them to be winners. Champions.

So Beau kicked himself into gear and went to get in the saddle to help round up her escaped horses. After all, life on a busy ranch didn't stop because he had a headache and a sore throat.

His phone went nuts as he jogged after Charlotte and Kenny, but he didn't bother to check it. Cowboys and cowgirls would be streaming into the stables in only a few seconds. Outside the nearest one, Kenny had a couple of horses saddled already, and he'd thrown Marlin's rope over a nearby tethering post.

Charlotte mounted her horse just as Beau took his reins from Kenny. "Thank you, Kenny."

"Are you with me?" Charlotte called over to him, her voice steady despite the urgency of the situation. He wondered what her pulse sounded like inside her own body, because his pounded like horse's hooves on hard-packed dirt.

"Yes," he said, and they went around the back of the cabins and rode toward the homestead and Brynn's horse-training facility.

As they arrived on the scene, Beau wasn't surprised to see Brynn in the saddle already and Pete coming toward them on his pretty cream-colored horse.

"It's like they're having a party," Brynn said, indicating the fields north of the facility. The sight of scattered horses grazing and galloping freely brought both tension and determination to the group, especially Beau's shoulders.

"Let's split up," Charlotte suggested, pointing to the north end of the field. "I'll take the west side. You head east. We'll meet in the middle." She wasn't asking, and she looked at Brynn and not Beau.

"We can at least keep them from spreading out even more," Beau said.

"How many are out?" Pete asked as another couple of cowboys rode up.

"About a dozen," Brynn said, and Beau scanned the fields again. He only saw four or five horses, not twelve.

His stomach vibrated with the familiar thrill of doing something exciting and having Charlotte as his partner made it even better. Just the fact that he was with her said something, as she'd been hiding from him all week.

"You and Charlotte go," Brynn said. "See if you can't close them off."

"Sounds like a plan." Beau turned his horse, and Charlotte made an equally expert move. They trotted off together, and he felt closer to her than he had all this week. "I'm headed east." He moved before she could reply, but he trusted her to handle her horse appropriately.

Brynn's horses didn't wear any gear, and Beau wasn't sure of any of their personalities. He didn't carry a rope, and he wasn't great at throwing one anyway. He could in a pinch, but he usually rode at the back of the pack and let the dogs and other cowboys with better arms do any roping necessary.

He whistled and Pepper streaked forward toward a horse that couldn't be more than thirteen hands tall. Maybe it wasn't fully grown yet, and it turned back toward Brynn's facility, where two people were setting up chutes to funnel the horses toward.

"Ruby," Beau yelled. "Chute."

The collie barked in a rare show of her voice, and she joined Pepper in helping to move the shorter pony toward the chutes. Beau stayed out of their way and edged over toward a pair of horses who seemed to be in a love-hate relationship with one another.

With his dogs busy, all Beau could do was try to let these equines know he was in charge, not them. "Aye, aye, aye!" He yipped at them, and they started to trot away from him. Fine with him, and he kept pushing them toward Charlotte.

She had three horses coming his way, and Beau edged further north to start pushing them south. In the distance, Pepper and Ruby had the young horse in the chute, and he whistled to call them back.

He couldn't help but watch Charlotte work. She moved with such grace and confidence, herding a particularly stubborn mare with a technique only someone with her patience could manage. He felt a pang of admiration—he had always loved how headstrong she was, even when it irritated him.

"I've got the dogs," he called over to her, and she raised her hand to indicate she'd heard him. "Go on, Pepper. Round 'em up. Ruby, chute."

Pepper barked and darted at the horses, which got them moving faster. A couple more dogs joined them from the ranch, and they got those five horses in the chute without a problem.

"Not sure where the others are," Charlotte said, and the buildings between them and where they'd left Brynn blocked Beau's view. "But there's one on that far fence." She nodded over her shoulder. "I think he thinks if he doesn't move, he's invisible."

"Ah," Beau said with a chuckle as he spotted the dark brown horse. "A cat-horse."

She burst out laughing, and Beau sure did like that. He wished he could reach over and take her hand in his, but they both needed both hands on their horses to maneuver. "We'll need to work together again," Charlotte said, her eyes sparkling with challenge.

"We're pretty good at that," Beau said. "Right?"

"Seem to be." She gave him a grin he hadn't seen all week either, and that gave his heart some courage. "You bring those dogs. They're incredible."

"And you thought they just existed to keep my feet warm at night."

She turned her horse as she giggled, and Beau went with her. "Come on, Pepper. Ruby. Spots and Garfield, let's go. We've got a horse back here." He rode toward the fence, the four dogs trotting alongside his horse.

Charlotte expertly moved to the left, and Beau guided his horse to the right. The runaway horse had pinned itself against a fence, and he'd have to go back toward the facility. He'd want to anyway, as Brynn took great care of her horses.

Charlotte reached him first, and she spoke softly, her words barely audible over the breeze, calming the horse. Beau watched her for a moment, then took his cue to slowly edge closer, offering a hand that the horse sniffed cautiously.

"Let's go, bud," Charlotte said. "Time to go home." She turned back toward the facility and simply walked away, clearly expecting the errant horse to follow her. As horses were herd animals and thrived with groups of their own kind, Beau was only kind of awed that the darker horse put his head down and simply went.

"All right, guys," Beau said. "Looks like we're just goin' back." His phone chimed, and he checked it, as he'd had to do so plenty of times while in the saddle. "Oh, Pete needs you guys over on the west side."

Beau looked that way, and he found a few mounted riders out that way. "Let's go." He swung his horse that way and called to Charlotte, "They need the dogs over there. I'm gonna go help."

"Okay," she said, waving as she did. He didn't want to ride away from her, but duty called, and Beau had become really good at fulfilling his duty over the years.

With so many out to help now, and the dogs being amazing herders, it didn't take long for Brynn to get all of her horses back behind sturdy fences. Beau returned to the stable, took care of his horse, and put him away.

"You okay, Kenny?" He didn't see Charlotte anywhere, but the horse she'd been riding had already been put away.

"We're good," he said. "Thanks, boss."

Beau stifled a cough as he headed home. He exited the stable and turned right, and when his house came into view, he found the lovely Charlotte sitting on the steps, seemingly waiting for him.

Oh, this was so much better than climbing those steps alone and entering a dark, silent, empty house. *So* much better.

She smiled when she saw him, and she lifted her hand in a silent hello. Beau climbed the steps and sat on the top one with her, a sigh escaping his mouth as he did. He'd forgotten to text around for the breakfast ingredients he needed, and he pulled out his phone to do that.

"I just need a few minutes to get what I need for dinner."

"You don't need to cook."

He looked over to her. "We have to eat, and I'm too tired to drive to town."

She linked her arm through his and leaned into his shoulder. Oh, he liked that, and he leaned his head against hers. "Charlotte, I'm scared."

"Of what?"

"Of falling in love with you and having my heart ripped out." Beau realized how ridiculous it sounded when he said it out loud. "So I've been a little flirtier this week. Less serious. And it's not what I want."

She said nothing, and that only made Beau's nerves vibrate with more tension. Then annoyance. "Are you going to say anything?"

Chapter Twenty

Charlotte wanted to get closer to Beau, but she didn't know how. "Yeah, I'm going to say something." As soon as she figured out what. Or how to make the things she felt in her heart turn into words she could utter.

Beau waited, because he was one of the most patient people on the planet. Except for this afternoon, though he had told her three times she needed to be done before he called her training session.

"I've been a little distant this week too," she said.

"You don't say."

She wanted to shut down, but she'd waited out here on these steps specifically to talk to him. "You're just so good at saying what you want to say."

"I'm not," he said.

"But I'm not," she continued. "And I started feeling all these things for you last week on your birthday, and it's confusing to me."

He let some silence pass through them, though plenty of people kept coming and going from the stable only thirty yards away. "What kinds of things are you feeling?"

"Same as you," she said, her heartbeat pumping hard.

"Oh, I'm gonna need to hear you say it," Beau teased.

Charlotte raised her head and looked at him. The smile dropped from his face instantly, his expression replaced with pure desire and flaming emotion. She swallowed, and said, "I've never told someone I love them."

"You shouldn't say it unless you mean it," he said. "And I didn't say I loved you, I said I was falling in that direction." He raised his eyebrows. "Are you saying the same thing? Because if you are, I think you should say it instead of just piggybacking on what I said."

His mouth twitched into a smile that didn't last long. Charlotte could dive into his eyes and stay there forever.

"I'm going to kiss you," he whispered. They hadn't been doing much of that this week, and the moment his lips touched hers, Charlotte realized how much she'd missed kissing him. How much she'd missed *him*, though he'd been living right across the hall from her.

Fireworks popped between them, and choirs of angels sang from heaven above. Charlotte had been sifting through abstract things in her bedroom the last few nights, and she still didn't know everything.

But as she kissed Beau on the front steps of their cabin, she finally let go of...everything. She let go of her fears. She let go of her stubbornness. She let go of her reservations, and she allowed herself to freefall.

"Mm, yep." Beau stopped kissing her, but he didn't pull away. "Definitely falling in love with you."

Charlotte still hadn't said the words, and her head felt so light, with a pair of very heavy lips as she said, "I'm falling in love with you too, Beau."

He laughed, a low chuckle that started in his chest and grew as it came out of his mouth. He turned his head away and covered his mouth as his laugh turned into a cough.

Compassion filled her, and she just wanted tonight to be easy on Beau. He'd been fighting a cold for days now.

"And there it is." He took her face in both of his hands, his eyes searching hers. "You okay? Is your heart freaking out?"

"No," she said. "But *I'm* freaking out."

Beau smiled and said, "I've already kissed you, and I'm afraid you're going to get sick now, but could we...go work on dinner? I'm beat, and I just want to lie down."

Charlotte got to her feet, feeling like someone had poured glitter and unicorn horns into her bloodstream. "Come lie down while I work on dinner."

"I was going to make dinner."

"Are we going to argue over this?" Charlotte took his hand and pretended to pull him to his feet. Like she could do that. They went inside together, and Charlotte hurried ahead of him to pull boxes of cereal out of the cupboard.

"I know what you want." She got out the milk and a carton of cream. "Just sit down and let me serve you."

Beau sat at the bar and watched as she poured half a bowl of Only-Berries and then added another half-bowl of Corn Chex. He started to chuckle, and that made Charlotte's heart happy and light. She pushed the bowl in front of him and got out a spoon.

"You pour your own milk and cream," she said.

"Just the fact that you know I like cream with this tells me something."

"Yeah? What does it tell you?"

"That you really are falling in love with me." Then he picked up the carton of cream and proceeded to pour *only* cream on his mixed cereal.

Withholding her judgment, she picked up the box of Special K Red Berries and poured a whole bowl for herself. Then she sat beside him and only added cream to her cereal too.

She met his eye and lifted her spoon as if to toast him. He clinked his spoon against hers, and that made her giggle, a giddiness parading through her that she couldn't squash no matter how she tried.

Maybe this was what love felt like. Charlotte wasn't sure, but she catalogued the feelings to analyze once Beau had taken some medicine and gone to bed.

Evenings later, Charlotte raised her head when someone knocked on the cabin door. Beau had already gone to bed, and Charlotte should be heading that direction herself. Instead, she moved Pepper off her feet—the dogs stayed with her until she gently opened Beau's door when she went to bed. Then, Pepper and Ruby went to sleep with their master—and got up.

The door opened as she rounded the couch, and while it surprised Charlotte, it didn't scare her. Especially not when she saw Kelly Ackerman entering with a huge pot in her hands.

"Hey," Charlotte said.

"We brought you dinner." She advanced toward Charlotte, who backed up to give her room. Squire came right behind her, carrying a plastic grocery sack in one hand and a big container of apple juice in the other.

"Beau loves apple juice," he said as he lifted it.

"I brought chicken tortellini soup," Kelly said. "Squire's got salad and rolls." She groaned as she lifted the obviously heavy pot onto the counter. "Should be good for a few days."

Squires wares joined Kelly's, and Charlotte looked at the food and then them. Gratitude filled her, and she stepped into Kelly's arms to hug her before she started crying. "Thank you."

"You've been eating cold cereal for days, haven't you?" Kelly laughed, but Charlotte didn't.

She stepped back and grinned. "It's just so nice to have someone else thinking about you." And not in a way that made her feel weak. Like her heart wasn't good enough to do anything.

"We know you haven't been to town and couldn't have much. Then Ben came and spied for us, and sure enough, he said y'all needed food." Kelly smiled at Squire. "Is Beau in bed already?"

Charlotte nodded. "He's going to the doctor tomorrow, finally. He's just not getting better, and the over-the-counter stuff isn't helping much."

"And you haven't gotten it?" Squire asked.

She shook her head. "So far, no. Thankfully." Charlotte had actually thanked the Lord she hadn't gotten whatever bug had bitten Beau. If she got sick, Mason would insist she come home and let Felicity nurse her back to health. Or maybe he wouldn't. Charlotte wasn't sure anymore.

They'd been getting along just fine since the incident in the feed store, and he hadn't been texting as much now that she thought of it. She simply hadn't noticed, because she didn't have the time or energy to deal with one more emotional thing. Who knew falling in love would be so time-consuming and an emotional rollercoaster?

Maybe it wasn't like that for everyone, but for Charlotte, it had been. So far.

"You and Beau are gettin' along?" Squire asked.

Kelly swatted his chest. "Squire, what a question."

"What?" he asked. "I'm just making sure everything is okay here."

"You made it sound weird."

Charlotte laughed, as she enjoyed their bickering. "Beau and I are getting along great," she said, glancing down the hallway like he might appear. "We had some rough spots, but we've smoothed them out."

"Beau is pretty smooth," Squire said with a smile.

"Okay, we're leaving," Kelly said.

"What did I say now?" Squire moved as she nudged him toward the door. "It's true. Beau is a cool cat."

"You made it sound like he's not real," Kelly said. "Charlotte, Beau is one of the most genuine, caring, hard-working men we have the privilege of knowing." She put both hands over her heart. "I swear."

Charlotte blinked at her. "I know that."

"See? She knows that," Squire tore his unhappy gaze from his wife and nodded to Charlotte. "We hope the food goes to good use."

"I've already eaten tonight, but I'm going to have some anyway," Charlotte said, putting on the best smile she owned. "Thank you so much, really. You've saved us from starvation."

Squire chuckled then, and he stepped out onto the porch. Kelly went with him, pulling the door closed behind her with a "Goodbye, Charlotte. We're so glad you're here at Three Rivers."

Charlotte stared at it for a moment, wondering what had just happened. "You were just reminded that you belong here," she said. Then she stepped over to the soup pot and lifted the lid. The scent of cream and herbs filled her nose and made her mouth water.

"Wow," she said to the dogs. "We are feasting tonight."

* * *

The following morning, Charlotte left her bedroom and glanced across the hall to Beau's. She'd done this every day since she'd moved in, and every day, his door had been open. He always got up ahead of her, as he had to get outside and stage himself for his Sunrise Cowboy broadcast.

Alarm tugged through her, because the sunrise couldn't be far away. True, it had started happening later and later in the morning, as they moved into the winter months—if Texas truly had any of those.

She'd been told the Panhandle did occasionally see snow, and Charlotte secretly hoped for that. But she knew Beau would be out there in the morning, doing his sunrise livestream, even in the bad weather.

So why wasn't he out there today?

She moved over to his door and twisted the knob quietly, just like she did to let the dogs into his room at night. They'd both gotten off the bed already to greet her, and she whispered, "Hey, guys. Go to the back door, and I'll let you out."

Both Pepper and Ruby trotted off, but Charlotte peered into the dark recesses of Beau's bedroom. She had not been inside it, not one time, and now, she clearly heard the soft, steady breathing of the cowboy she lived with.

He had not gotten up, but he was clearly still alive.

A wild idea formed in her head, as quickly as tornadoes formed and touched down. She stole across the room to his nightstand and picked up his phone. He kept his tripod in the loft, and Charlotte left as quickly as she'd come, and she closed his door behind him.

With the dogs waiting for her at the back door, she went up into the loft and got the tripod. "You can't go out in your pajamas."

Moving fast now so she could beat the sun, she dashed to the back door and opened it for the dogs. Then she flew back down the hall to her bedroom, where she shed her silky pjs in favor of jeans and a sweatshirt.

"You don't have to be on camera," she said. "You just have to find a place to film the sunrise and talk about the ranch."

She knew what Beau did, because she watched him every single morning. He'd even called her out once or twice, naming her as his girlfriend.

Calling her his.

Her heart pounded and swooped to the soles of her feet. "Calm down." She took a big breath and tried to slow everything in her body as she pulled on her running shoes. Then she grabbed his phone and the tripod and followed the dogs outside.

She had no idea if Beau planned his sunrise shots or not. In her mind, the prettiest place would be on the other side of the stables, with a shot of the pastures Courage Reins used for their horses.

For Charlotte, it always came down to horses.

It wasn't completely dark, and she couldn't whistle like Beau, but she did her best to call the dogs as she hustled toward what she felt certain would be the perfect place for the Sunrise Cowgirl to do her first live-stream.

Chapter Twenty-One

Beau woke up to sunlight streaming into his eyes. Disoriented, he shot straight up, his pulse knocking against the back of his tongue. "Where—?" He recognized his bedroom then, though he rarely saw it in such glorious light.

And Pepper and Ruby were absent. He immediately turned to pick up his phone to see what time it was—and it wasn't there.

Now feeling completely discombobulated because of the loss of his device—the thing he used to keep track of everything from the name of Charlotte's heart condition to how much he owed Bennett for groceries—Beau stumbled to his feet.

His head positively pounded, and he sank back to the mattress. He couldn't make sense of much more than the pain in his head, but he knew one thing: He'd missed the sunrise.

Disappointment cut through him like a hot, sharp knife. He hadn't missed his sunrise live-stream in *years*. He hadn't posted that he wouldn't be there, and he wondered for a brief moment if anyone actually cared.

His thoughts cleared, the way thunderclouds dissipated after they'd dropped their rain. "Of course people care," he said, echoing the voice in his head saying the same thing. "People care about you, Beau."

Just because he was forty and unmarried didn't mean he didn't matter.

He got to his feet again, and he managed to pull on a T-shirt and a pair of jeans. He made it into the kitchen, where the clock on the microwave told him it had just passed nine o'clock.

"Oh, boy, Beau," he said to himself, trying to remember what day it even was. Did he have a meeting this morning? Assignments to hand out? Why hadn't anyone awakened him?

"And where's Charlotte? And my phone?"

She'd retreated, but he'd thought they'd made great progress in the past few days. Why wasn't she here? "She could've at least left me a note," he grumbled.

As if summoned by his questions, the front door opened, and Charlotte walked in. "Hey, you're awake." She smiled like he slept past nine every day. "I was just coming to see if you wanted to shower before I take you to the doctor."

"Take me to the doctor?"

"Yes." She held out her hand, and in it, she had his phone.

He practically lunged for it, and Charlotte stepped back, her eyebrows up. "Did I miss a lot?"

"No," she said simply. "I handled it."

He looked at his phone, where he did not have a single

message. Not one missed call. No texts. Nothing. Disbelief stormed through him now, and he could barely swallow. That could be because of his fiery throat, but whatever.

"You handled it? You handled what, exactly?"

"Your voice sounds bad. Do you want some apple juice?" She went past him and to the fridge.

"Apple juice? We don't have apple juice."

"Squire and Kelly brought some last night." She pulled it out, and nothing had looked so good. "Your doctor's appointment is in an hour and a half, and yes, I'm taking you. It's an executive decision I reached with Bennett, when he learned you hadn't gotten up for your sunrise live-stream."

"I can drive myself."

"Nevertheless." She passed him the glass of apple juice. "I texted Squire to say you were too ill to work today, and he said he'd make sure everything was covered. Then I fed the horses, so they're all happy as larks." She grinned at him like this was their new normal.

But it couldn't be. He took a sip of the apple juice, his whole mouth rejoicing. The sip turned into a swallow, and then a gulp.

Charlotte laughed lightly. "You did get a lot of messages this morning on the live-stream. I had to mute the app, because it was driving me nuts."

He set down his glass. "Messages on the live-stream?"

She nodded, somewhat sober now. "I did it for you. I didn't want you to miss a day; I know how important it is to you." She reached up and tightened her ponytail, a show of her nerves. "I was pressed for time, but I managed to make it over to the donkeys before the sun really came up. I think I did okay. You'll have to watch it and give me a critique."

Oh, he wasn't going to do that. Watch her live-stream on his channel, yes. But critique it? No way.

He put his phone in his back pocket, and with his heart swelling past its bounds, he let the things he felt for Charlotte expand and grow until they burst beyond his body. He gathered her right into his arms and pressed a messy and firm kiss to her lips.

"You did my live-stream for me."

"Yes," she said, a slight gasp coming with the word.

He searched her face, trying to find the words he wanted. They came, but he bucked against them, because he'd never said them out loud to a woman before, and he had no idea what response he'd get.

"You fed the dogs."

"Yes."

"You texted Squire."

"That's right."

"You and Bennett decided I needed a babysitter at the doctor?"

Charlotte smiled a little then and reached up to cradle his face. "I know you don't need me to take care of you, cowboy. But I think it's okay if I *want* to."

He'd said exactly that to her too, and Beau's whole being filled with another round of love. "I love you, little bird."

Her eyes widened, and then she did the most remarkable thing. She said, "I love you too, Beau."

Chapter Twenty-Two

Charlotte pulled up to the cabin and looked over to Beau. "I've never driven you to town and back."

He didn't lift his head from the rest as he turned it to look at her. "Thank you, Charlotte."

"We got everything, so let's get you in bed." She reached down and picked up her purse, where she'd put his antibiotic and the few groceries she'd run in to buy while he'd napped in the SUV.

Beau was still handsome though he looked ragged around the edges. Walking pneumonia would do that to a person, she supposed. "Come on," she said when he didn't move. "The doctor said lots of fluids, rest, and to let me take care of you."

He said nothing, but he got out of the vehicle. She met him at the front and went inside with him. "Go get changed. I'll sort through the meds and bring you everything."

Beau pressed a kiss to the side of her neck, which made her smile and startle at the same time. "Thank you, little bird." He went down the hall, and Charlotte focused on the cough medicine—needed for sleeping—the antibiotic, and a nasal spray.

"And he needs painkillers," she said. She opened all the bags of prescriptions and set the little bottles in a row. She got him an antibiotic and a couple of ibuprofen pills, as well as one of his cough medicine capsules.

She poured a glass of apple juice and pulled out the buffalo chicken wrap she'd bought at the grocery store for his lunch. Down the hall, she knocked on his door. Pepper barked at the same time Beau said, "Come in."

Charlotte entered with the food and pills to find Beau propped up in bed. He had his phone, but he lowered it, his face softening when he saw her. She slid the plate onto his nightstand and held out her hand with the pills in it.

He took them and lifted the apple juice glass to his lips, swallowing everything without a single question.

"You have to eat with those," she said. "Or you'll be sick."

"Yes, ma'am." He didn't immediately reach for the wrap, but instead, he looked at her with glinting, mischievous eyes. "Come watch your live-stream with me."

A blip of unrest fired through Charlotte, and then she reminded herself it hadn't been that bad. She'd been a little stilted in the beginning, because she didn't have Beau's easy charm and quick wit. But she'd done a decent job.

So she went around to the other side of his bed and climbed onto it with him. She stayed over the covers as she cuddled into his side and he held up his phone so they could both see it.

"Okay, I think it's working," she said on the screen. It

showed the pastures in front of her, Beau's three donkeys, and the barns and stables past that. The sky still held a horrible pre-dawn gray, so she hadn't missed it.

"Let me know if you can see our sunrise from the Texas Panhandle, here at Three Rivers Ranch. Then I'll know if I got it going right."

Emojis of hearts and thumbs-up started flying up the screen, and Charlotte grinned. "I was so relieved when I saw those."

"Oh, praise the Lord," she said on the live-stream. "Sorry to those of you looking for the Sunrise Cowboy. Beau is a little under the weather this morning, but I know he wouldn't want you to miss the sunrise here in our corner of the world."

She continued talking about where she'd set up and why, pointing out Tilly, Sprout, and Jasper, then the stables where she worked as the Stable Manager. She answered the questions that flew by, and she told them about this perfect autumn morning at Three Rivers Ranch.

After about twenty-five minutes, she ended the broadcast, the same way she'd seen and heard Beau do before. "Until tomorrow's sunrise," she said. "Have a good one, doing good things and living good lives."

She ended the livestream without shaking the phone, and she laid her head against Beau's chest. "I did okay, I think."

"Okay?" he asked. "Sweetheart, you killed that live-stream. It was incredible." He pressed a kiss to her temple. "Thank you for doing it for me."

"I almost fainted getting everything going," she said. "I was so rushed and afraid I was going to miss it."

"You really almost fainted, or you were just nervous?"

Charlotte paused for a moment. "I think a little of both, actually."

"Well, I'd have been mad if you'd have really passed out over a sunrise."

"It wasn't just a sunrise, cowboy."

Beau hesitated for just a moment. "What was it then? To you?"

Charlotte took a few seconds to think about that. "I'm not sure," she said. "I don't know how to explain it. I just didn't want the live-stream not to happen. It's important to you, so it became important to me, and I don't know."

Beau said nothing, which was his way of telling her to keep talking.

"I liked doing the live-stream too," she admitted. "No one knew anything I didn't tell them. I felt invisible, but in a good way. I'm not the same stubborn, headstrong woman who came here with something to prove."

"Mm." He kissed her again. "I think you're still a little stubborn and headstrong, but in a good way now."

She let her eyes drift closed, because he was right and she was so comfortable with him. "I think I'll always be like that, but I'm working on my temper and listening to others and you know. Things."

"Yeah? Why's that?"

"Because," she said. "I think I've proven what I wanted to prove, and now I just want to care for the horses here, and continue to be part of this ranch, and...."

The last thing had to do with Beau, and while she'd told

him she loved him only a few hours ago, a sudden shyness came over her.

"And be with you," she finally finished. "I want to be yours, and I know I have to keep working on myself so we can be together."

"Baby, I think you're amazing."

"I know you do," she said. "You've always been so support-ive, and I appreciate that. I...well, to be honest, I don't know how to be a good girlfriend. I don't have much experience with it."

"What about a wife?" he asked. "Do you think you could be that? Be *my* wife?"

"Well, now, you're making my heart freak out."

He chuckled lightly and tightened his arm around her. "Something to think about, then. I know you like to take some time to do that before you say anything."

"Yeah."

"I've changed a little too," he said.

"You have?"

"Yeah, I think so." He drew in a breath that lifted his chest where her head lay. "I used to be this flirty, dance-with-and-date-anyone guy. I still love to laugh and flirt, but I really only want to do any of that with you. I want to make you smile and laugh. I want to hear you say my name or call me *cowboy*. I one-hundred percent want to be your husband and have you be my wife, but I'm not in a rush."

"No?"

"I've waited forty years," he said. "I can wait a little longer, until we're both ready."

Charlotte wrapped her arm across his midsection. "If we get married, what color will your bowtie be?"

Beau laughed, which turned to coughing, and Charlotte sat up. "Sorry," she said. He shook his head, and Charlotte slid off the bed and went around to his side. "You need to rest. I'm going to go eat and get back to work. I'll check on you in an hour."

He quieted and met her eyes. "One more thing."

"No more things," she said firmly. "Only napping."

"Are you going to tell Mason we just talked about getting married? Or am I?"

Charlotte's blood seemed to turn into a solid, but thankfully it only lasted for a single moment. "I talked to him a bit ago. He knows it's coming." She sighed. "Honestly, he's going to be happy for us, don't you think?"

"I think your brother is unpredictable," he said with a smile. "Maybe it runs in the family."

"Okay, I'm going." Charlotte turned and walked away from him as he protested and tried to get her to come back. She turned at the doorway and added, "I'm taking your dogs with me. They don't have pneumonia."

"Don't go mad."

"I'm not mad."

"We can tell him together."

She nodded, her chest a little too tight still. "I'll text Felicity and set up dinner for a couple of weeks from now. You should be better then."

"Sounds great." He grinned at her, his flirty cowboy persona in full force. "Come kiss me good-bye, little bird."

Charlotte did love kissing him, and she'd been doing it plenty while he'd been sick. So she crossed back to him and let him gather her into his arms to kiss her. "I can't wait to make you mine," he whispered, his lips catching on hers.

And because Charlotte wanted that too, she said, "I can't wait for that either."

Then she left him to rest, and she took Pepper and Ruby out to the stables with her, where she went down every aisle and sang to every horse about how she and Beau were going to get married someday.

Once they'd all heard her songs and lullabies, she pulled out her phone and texted Felicity about her and Beau coming to dinner in a couple of weeks.

Chapter Twenty-Three

Beau reached into his closet and pulled out the two-by-four holding all the bowties he'd worn to various weddings here on the ranch.

He'd actually been to a lot more—all the Glover Family weddings, the Walker cowboys. He'd been to their weddings too.

"So many weddings," he said. "So many memories." They flooded his mind, and all of them were good, as if God had washed away the bitter and jealous feelings Beau had endured during some of the ceremonies, dinners, parties, and dances.

"Beau," Bennett called, and Beau twisted toward his bedroom door.

"In my room."

Bennett entered several seconds later, by which time Beau had put the row of bowties on the bed. He looked away from it and toward Bennett. "Hey, brother." He hugged his best friend and together, they looked at the wedding wear.

"What's goin' on here?" Bennett asked.

"I'm getting rid of the bowties," Beau said. "Every time I open my closet to get dressed, they mock me."

"I thought you and Charlotte were getting serious."

"Yeah." Beau nodded, his smile starting in his soul before it reached his face. "We are. Real serious."

Harvest had come and gone, and they'd survived him stumbling home late and getting up early. They'd done the sunrise live-stream together a few times, and Charlotte had done it for him three more times, simply to give him another hour of sleep.

"I'm going to town to get the ring this afternoon," Beau said. "And I don't want these here anymore."

"Then let's get rid of them." Bennett reached for the first one and plucked it from the board. "And you got her a ring?" He gave Beau a side-eyed look that broadcasted his surprise. "That's huge, Beau. *Really* huge."

"Never bought a diamond ring before," Beau acknowledged. He started picking off the bowties from the other end of the board, the more recent weddings. Ben's wasn't on here, as Beau hadn't had space for it, and he didn't want to display a token of another wedding he'd attended as a single man.

It only took a minute to get all the bowties off the board, and he crammed the ones he'd collected into Ben's hands. "You do it."

"What do you want me to do with them?"

"I don't know. Don't we have some trash to burn on the ranch today?"

"Not with the fire danger being in the red," Ben said. "You know what, Beau? This is easy. They're trash, so we put them in the trashcan." He turned and left the bedroom, and while he was gone disposing of the bowties, Beau removed all the tags and pictures marking which wedding belonged to which garment.

When Ben returned, all he had was a two-by-four, and Beau knew what to do with that. He gave the tags and pictures to Ben, and they left the bedroom, Beau carrying the long board. Charlotte had gone out to the stables already, so she wasn't there for his bowtie cleansing, which was just fine with Beau.

He'd barely wanted Bennett to come, but he'd asked him to come over for a little "housekeeping," and to go pick up Charlotte's ring with him. Somehow, even as a forty-year-old, Beau needed a little hand-holding with the purchase.

Plus, he'd gone with Ben when he'd bought Ellie's ring. It felt fitting, and like what Beau wanted to be doing. They'd get lunch first, then head to the jewelers, and Beau had told Charlotte that he and Ben were going to lunch and picking up ranch supplies.

They had to do that too, so it wasn't a lie.

He watched Ben toss the tags in the trashcan in the kitchen, and then they took the board out to the barn where they kept scrap lumber. Beau dusted off his hands and looked at Ben. "Well? Ready?"

"Yes, sir." Ben grinned at him and threw his arm around him. "I can't believe you're getting married." He laughed, and Beau knew he wasn't teasing. It really just was joyful.

Beau grinned and stumbled under the weight of Ben's arm. "I know, right? I can barely believe it."

"Charlotte's amazing," Ben said. "I really like her, Beau."

"And the best part is, she won't have to move after we get married." He grinned at Ben, who shook his head as he chuckled.

"Oh, she'll be movin', brother," Ben said. "I mean, she's not gonna live across the hall from you once you guys say 'I do.'" He raised his eyebrows. "Right?"

Beau had not allowed himself to think about walking into a bedroom he shared with Charlotte. But now he did. "Yeah," he said quietly.

"Marriage is the best," Ben said.

"Yeah?" Beau asked. "Are you and Ellie gonna have kids right away?" They'd already been married for a few months now, but Beau hadn't gotten any announcements.

Ben's face fell. "I'm not sure about that," he said. "Ellie's been having some health issues." He flashed a smile at Beau that held more pain than happiness. "She might not be able to carry a baby. She's been goin' to the doctor for only a month or so. We don't know much yet."

Beau's whole body turned to lead. "I'm sorry, Ben."

"We don't know much yet," he repeated. He tried on another smile. "I'm trying to stay positive, and Ellie doesn't want anyone to know quite yet."

"Of course," Beau said. "I won't say anything to anyone."

They piled into his truck, and Beau started the drive to town. He and Ben were so close and had been through so much, that he didn't expect Ben to wallow in silence and sorrow, and he didn't.

They started talking about the upcoming holiday festivities on the ranch, and Ben said, "I hope Squire and Kelly have another multi-ranch party. That ugly sweater contest was a hoot." He laughed, and Beau joined in.

"Sure was," he said. But he hadn't heard head nor tail of a Christmas party, though Kelly could definitely put together a meal and a get-together faster than the weather changed in Texas. "I'm headed to Preacher's for a Friendsgiving next month," he said. "Me and Charlotte. They want to meet her."

"Yeah, I'm sure they do."

"Why don't you and Ellie come with?" He glanced over to Ben. "I know her sister lives here, but it's a Friendsgiving. We'll go to Charlotte's for Thanksgiving Day, but this is the Saturday following."

Ben's face lit up. "Do you think I'm invited?"

"Yes," Beau said without missing a beat. "You've met the Glovers, right? They won't care at all. I'll call Preacher right now."

"Don't do that," Ben said. "Just ask him later. But I think Ellie would like that. She was saying that all we do is drive out here, work, drive home, and collapse in bed."

Beau laughed. "It's just busy right now," he said. "Fall always is."

"Sure is." Ben sighed as he leaned his seat back. "I'm gonna take a nap, so maybe I can stay up past eight o'clock tonight."

Beau grinned over to him, and he let Bennett have his nap. They enjoyed lunch, and then Beau found himself opening the door of the jeweler where he hoped to find a ring for Charlotte. They'd talked a little bit more about a wedding and marriage, but Beau hadn't come right out and asked her what kind of ring she'd like.

Charlotte didn't wear any jewelry that Beau had seen—maybe a small pair of earrings on his birthday. But no rings, bracelets, or necklaces. A lot of cowgirls didn't, so he smiled at the woman who approached him and Ben and said, "I need a ring for a woman who works with horses and probably won't wear it much."

The woman didn't miss a beat and her smile didn't slip a centimeter as she said, "We have sets where she can wear one when possible, like to church or when she's not working, and when she can't, it can be worn on a chain around her neck."

Beau wasn't sure Charlotte would even do that. He didn't care. The diamond ring wasn't the thing that made her his. The way she relaxed around him did that. The way she kissed him and gave herself to him—mind and body and soul—did that.

"All right," he said, and he went with her to look at rings. Within only a few minutes, he got overwhelmed with settings and cuts and gold versus white gold. Thankfully, Ben was there to ask questions, and after a half-hour, he looked at Beau.

"Which one do you like?"

"Is it about me?"

"Yeah, which one do you like for Charlotte?"

"Beau?"

He turned in the direction of the familiar voice, and he found Mason entering the jewelry shop. "Hey, Mace." He moved over to his college best friend and man-clap-hugged him. "You made it."

He scanned the jewelry cases in front of him, his eyes landing on Ben for a moment, and then the saleswoman for another. He then switched his eagle-eyed gaze to Beau. "You're buying a ring for my sister."

"Yes, sir." Beau grinned and rocked back on his heels. "We've looked at a lot, and I've narrowed it down to three. I'd love your help in choosing one."

"You've picked three?" Mason asked, seemingly determined to be grumpy. "Where are they?"

"I'm getting them now." Beau went back down the counter with the saleswoman, and he pointed out the three rings he liked best. The three he hoped *Charlotte* would like the best. She set each of them on a black velvet tray and set them in front of Beau, Ben, and Mason.

Mason whistled and said, "Whoo-ee, Beau. You can afford these?"

"Yes," Beau said without further explanation. "Mason, I'm in love with your sister, and she loves me."

Mason looked at him fully then, maybe for the first time since he'd moved to Three Rivers, despite the dinner he and Charlotte had gone to a couple of weeks ago. He searched Beau's face, and he apparently found what he was looking for.

Everything about him softened, and oh, Beau had seen that

exact same thing happen to Charlotte. They really were cut from the same DNA.

"I see that." Mason slung his arm around Beau's shoulders. "All right then, brother. I'd go with this one." He pointed out the middle ring, the one with the smallest diamond and the most white gold. "My sister doesn't like gold, and she's not flashy. She just wants to be seen and appreciated, and this will convey that just fine."

"I like that one too," Ben said.

Beau didn't want to hem and haw. He wanted this job done, so he could move on to the next thing: Asking Charlotte to be his wife.

"That's the one then," he said to the saleswoman. "Oh, and I did get her ring size." He tapped to open his phone, where he'd noted it after Felicity had gotten it for him. "It's a seven."

While she went through the paperwork and started checking him out, Beau looked at the two men with him. "Thank you both," he said.

"Of course," Ben said while Mason barked out a "Yep." He gave Beau a squinted look and then started to smile, then laugh. "I can't believe I came to town to do *this*."

Beau grinned back at him. "And you're not done yet. Now, I'm going to need some help with this proposal...."

* * *

Beau pulled up to Mason's mansion on his million-dollar ranch, a familiar pinch of jealousy making his lungs tight.

When he didn't get out and grab the bags of salad they'd brought to contribute to the meal, Charlotte hesitated too.

"Do you really want to be with me?" Beau asked as she looked at him.

"What kind of question is that?"

"It's a real one," he said, watching the house. "Look at this place. I'm not this, Charlotte. I have a cabin that isn't mine, on a ranch that isn't mine."

"I want everything you have," she said firmly. "Beau."

The use of his name got him to turn and look at her. She gave him a pretty smile with those pink, pink lips. "I don't want a big ranch that I have to run. Can you imagine me hosting lunches and holiday parties and being friends with all the cowboys?"

Beau smiled at her, but he felt tired. "No, ma'am."

"No, ma'am is right." She reached into the back seat and picked up their grocery bag of salads. "Now, let's go. The wind is howling, and I just want to be inside for the next few hours."

He followed her inside, and they entered the homestead together, Charlotte calling, "We're here."

Beau's heart started to freak out, and if he had her health condition, he felt certain he'd be slumping to the floor right this moment. He swallowed when he saw Charlotte's only nephew.

"Beau," the boy said. "Come see the new kittens."

"Oh, boy," he said. "They were born?"

"Last night," Felicity said as she entered the living room with a smile. "Hey, you two." She beamed at them with only sunshine in her soul, and she hugged him and Charlotte at the same time.

"Where did Tabby have them?" Charlotte asked.

"Guess." Felicity sounded unamused. "I told Mason we'll have to get a washer and dryer in the barn or something, because there's no way Tabby's letting me do laundry while her kittens are in there." She rolled her eyes and turned around. "Come get a drink and have some appetizers. Dinner will be in about a half-hour."

Beau detoured into the laundry room with Garrett to see the kittens, and they were definitely newborn cats as they didn't have their eyes open yet, and they mewed with the most pathetic voices. Still, he held the one Garrett gave him, and he looked at the boy. "We're all set?"

"Yes, sir," Garrett said. "Daddy says you're all set."

Beau smiled at him, gently handed the kitten back, and said, "All right. We better get this show on the road then."

It had been a couple of months since he'd first told Charlotte he loved her, but they'd dated so fast, and she needed a little more time to come to the same decisions he had, that he hadn't rushed into an engagement. She hadn't said a single word to him about it either.

She didn't know he'd bought a ring weeks ago, and she didn't know that he hoped to sit down to dinner in less than thirty minutes an engaged man.

Please let her say yes, he begged God, though Beau didn't really think Charlotte would say no.

He left the kittened laundry room and entered the main room of the mansion, which was a big combo room with a kitchen, living room and dining room. Charlotte's parents had come from the Hill Country, and Beau hadn't met them yet.

Charlotte swooped toward him and linked her arm through his. "My heart is freaking out," she whispered.

"I've got you, little bird," he whispered back. "I should be the nervous one. They already know you." His eyes darted around, and he caught her momma looking at him. "Introduce me."

Charlotte took a deep breath, and with her hand tight in through his arm, she led him over to where her momma sat at the dining room table, braiding together yellow, orange, red, and brown papers to make a chain with her granddaughter.

"Ella, I'm going to interrupt, okay? Beau hasn't met Grandma yet." Charlotte leaned into him, and Beau looked at her. She didn't seem pale, but that didn't mean much. "Momma, this is Beau Peterson. Beau, my momma, Linda." She nodded across the table to her daddy, who had a cup of steaming coffee in front of him. "And my daddy, David."

"Oh, Beau." Her momma swept up onto her feet and grabbed onto Beau. "It's so wonderful to meet you. Char has told us so much."

He laughed, putting on his meeting-parents skin. He had done this before, though not for a while. "Has she now?"

"So many good things." Linda stepped back and shone her light right on her. "Dave, come meet Beau."

Her daddy stood and leaned across the table. "Good to meet you, son."

"You too," Beau said. "I'm so glad to finally meet both

y'all." He smiled at everyone, and then looked at the braided chains. "Ella, are those ready?"

She looked at him, her face turning bright red. With wide eyes, she said, "All ready."

"Why don't we hang them up?" Linda asked, and she slid Beau a knowing look too. He glanced at Charlotte to see if she noticed her family acting kind of off. She didn't seem to, and she helped Kennedy start to clean up the paper strips.

Beau stepped out of the way and let Ella take one end of the strips to her grandfather while Mason opened a high cupboard in the kitchen to let down the banner he'd taken a picture of and sent to Beau.

He swallowed, suddenly scared out of his mind. Then Felicity met his eyes, and she nodded with so much encouragement in her smile that Beau's fears flew away. He followed everyone over to the setup they'd done for him and stood in front of them.

"Charlotte," he said into the silence, and she lifted her head from the table. She stilled when she saw her whole family standing with him, the Thanksgiving decorations behind him.

"Get down on your knees," Mason hissed, and Beau dropped to his knees.

He held out his hand for the diamond and Felicity handed him the black velvet box. He cracked it open and looked at Charlotte. "How's your heart, little bird?"

"Um." She looked over to her mom, but Beau didn't dare look away from her in case he lost his nerve.

"I hope it belongs to me," he said. "Because if it does, I promise you I'm going to take real good care of it. Because I love you, and I want you to live in my cabin with me, only in the same room."

Charlotte started to cry, and Beau had not anticipated that. He hadn't prepared a speech, because he'd never really had a problem saying what he wanted to say. Or what he felt.

"I love you with my whole heart, little bird. Will you marry me?"

Charlotte sniffled and clenched her fingers together. She needed time to think and collect her response, and Beau wasn't too concerned yet.

"Charlotte," her momma said.

"It's okay," Beau said. "She's almost there."

Charlotte looked at the banner and decoration behind him. "You made a banner for me."

He grinned at her as her eyes finally came to his.

"It has a little bird on it."

"It sure does." He'd had Charlie Glover help him get in touch with a graphic designer who'd made a banner with a pair of hands cradling a little bird. Then, he'd asked her nieces and nephew to make a chain of Thanksgiving colors that read, "Marry me."

And he'd enlisted her family to be there, minus the two brothers who couldn't travel for the holiday.

She rushed at him and fell to the ground in front of him. "I love you, Beau."

"You sure do." He nudged the ring box into her hand. "What do you think? Do you want be my wife?"

Her eyes searched his, and he loved the moment they lit

with everything she held so dear. "Yes," she whispered. "I really want to be your wife."

"And there it is." He took the ring out of the box, and since his forty-year-old knees begged him to get up, he'd explain about the necklace later. He slid it on her finger and met her eyes again. "There. You're mine."

She grinned and took his face in her hands. "Yes, I am, and you're mine, cowboy." Then she kissed him while her family whooped and hollered and cheered behind them.

Six Months Later

Charlotte ran her fingers down the strap that went over her right shoulder. She'd loved this dress upon first sight, as it had bright flowers, hummingbirds, other small birds, and honeybees flitting around the blooms stitched into the creamy-white fabric that encircled the skirt and floated up toward the bright blue belt around her waist.

She currently sat in a room at Courage Reins that she'd toured earlier. Beau had been a fixture at Three Rivers Ranch for so long that he wanted to get married here. Charlotte had felt like she belonged here the moment she'd stepped foot onto this land, so she hadn't had any qualms about saying her nuptials here.

They'd chosen May for the wedding, as the weather was usually pretty good without the major summer heat and without the spring rain. The day had dawned with a glorious sunrise she and Beau had broadcast together. He'd then told his viewers that they'd be gone for the next week, and Bennett would be taking over the Texas Panhandle sunrises until they returned from their honeymoon.

She'd wanted to see the beach, and Beau had arranged a trip for them to the Gulf Coast in Florida. Excitement built inside her again, and she couldn't believe she sat in a bride's room with her momma and Felicity, waiting to be led down to the big red barn where she would be married.

"Oh, don't cry," Felicity said. "This is the happiest day of your life." She hugged her around the shoulders and smiled at her in the mirror in front of them. "I just got notified that Beau's on his way to the altar."

Charlotte nodded, a baseball of emotions lodged in her throat. "What if I can't say my vows?" she managed to ask. "I'm so emotional." And she hated it. She shook her hands, trying to get some of the tension and anxiety to leave her body.

"Dear Lord," Charlotte prayed. "I want this to be a good day." She just needed to calm down. Her pulse raced, and she needed it to just *calm down*.

She took a deep breath and turned toward Felicity. "How's my hair?"

"Perfect," she said. "The flower crown matches the dress so perfectly."

Charlotte nodded and she rose and took Felicity into a hug. "Thank you for helping me with all the wedding prep. It's so beautiful, and it's because of you."

Felicity laughed and said, "I think I've found my calling. I absolutely loved planning this wedding with you."

"Charlotte," her mother said. "It's time."

She nodded and she moved in her bright blue heels toward the door where her momma waited. "You are beautiful and strong," her mom said, and that brought fresh pinch of emotion to Charlotte's chest.

Now, she just needed to get through the vows, and then Beau would kiss her, and everything would be well.

Charlotte went with her momma and Felicity, down the hall to the big glass windows that fronted the building. She stepped out into the warm May sunshine, her heels clicking softly against the concrete sidewalk and then the hard-packed dirt as she approached the barn.

The big white doors stood open, inviting her into a space transformed into rustic elegance. Strings of fairy lights twinkled from the rafters, casting a soft glow over the rows of wooden benches adorned with wildflowers, which mimicked the floral motif on her dress.

At the end of the aisle, beneath a floral arch, stood Beau, those beautiful eyes shining with anticipation. With hope. With absolute adoration.

For her, and Charlotte used it to quiet her pulse.

She waited while the wedding party went ahead of her, Pepper and Ruby—adorned with floral collars—leading Bennett and Ellie at the front of the pack.

Charlotte kept her arm in her father's, so glad she had a solid anchor to hold to. She wasn't going to pass out. She really wasn't.

Her eyes met Beau's again now that the wedding party had made it to the altar and then taken their seats.

As she began her walk, each guest looked at her, their

smiles wide and welcoming, adding warmth to her fluttering heart. At the end of the aisle, she stepped into the strong, gaping embrace of her brother.

"He is perfect for you," he whispered. "I'm sorry it took me so long to see it, but I do, Char." He stepped back, his intense gaze burning hotter than ever. "I really do."

She nodded, and moved to hug her mother and Felicity, though they'd embraced several times already. She stepped back to her father, who took her the last couple of steps to Beau. He passed her hand from his arm to Beau's, and now she had her forever anchor.

Her forever love.

Her forever cowboy.

Charlotte took a deep breath, looking into Beau's eyes. He smiled and whispered, "Are you freaking out?"

She shook her head, and said, "Just my heart is." She looked down at his bright blue bowtie. It matched the thread in her dress, her belt, and her heels, and he looked like a million bucks wearing it. "Nice bowtie."

"Thanks," he said. "I think I'm gonna keep this one." He chuckled and together they faced the pastor. His presence was her rock, his love the steady force that had guided her to this moment.

"Weddings are my favorite part of my job," the pastor began, his voice resonating in the barn's open space. "We are gathered here today to witness the union of Charlotte and Beau, a couple whose love story is as vibrant and enduring as the ranch they call home."

Charlotte listened, her heart swelling with each word, each promise of a future together. When it was her turn to speak her vows, she drew a deep, steadying breath. The crowd faded away until it was just her and Beau under the arch.

Just her and Beau in that cabin.

Just her and Beau, ready to tackle life together.

"Beau," she began, her voice trembling not at all. "Standing here with you, I feel like the luckiest woman in the world. You are my partner, my protector, and my best friend. I had no idea what love was or what it felt like, but you were so patient with me as I learned it's more than a feeling—it's a commitment, a decision to support and cherish each other through every sunrise and sunset."

Beau's eyes glistened with unshed tears as she continued, her voice growing stronger. "I vow to love you for who you are and who you will become, to respect you, and to grow with you. Together, we'll build a life with dogs and cats and horses and donkeys that feels like a never-ending adventure, and I can't wait to see where this journey takes us next. I promise to stand by your side, to laugh with you, and to comfort you in times of sorrow. And most of all, I promise to be true to us, to our dreams, and to our family here at Three Rivers Ranch."

As she spoke her vows, the tension melted away, replaced by a profound joy. She saw mirrored in Beau's expression the depth of his love, an unspoken promise that they were in this together, forever.

Beau took her hands in his, his voice steady and sure. "Charlotte, from the moment I saw you standing in my cabin, you changed everything. You brought light into my life and joy into my heart. I promise to cherish you, to protect you, and to be your partner in all things. I vow to make you laugh when you're taking life too seriously and to hold you close on the cold nights."

He grinned in that self-assured, sexy, flirty way he had and said, "I love you, my little bird, and I will with my whole heart, my entire soul, for today and all of my tomorrows."

He nodded, and she was surprised her vows were a little longer than his. Still, he'd said all the right things, and they faced the pastor to finish the ceremony.

The pastor pronounced them husband and wife, and as Beau dipped her for their first kiss as a married couple, cheers erupted around them. Pepper barked joyfully, adding to the celebration. A surge of happiness so intense it seemed to lift her off her feet bolted through Charlotte, and she couldn't quite kiss Beau—not with her smile so big and laughter leaking from her mouth.

He finally righted her, and they faced the crowd. Beau bellowed—of course—and he lifted their joined hands in victory. Charlotte laughed along with him, and she stepped over to his momma and gripped her in a hug while he double-embraced his two sisters.

They went down the aisle and out into the evening sunshine. They'd head over to the pasture for dinner and dancing, where tents had been set up to protect them from the elements. She'd wanted dinner with donkeys and horses, and Beau had spent the past week cleaning the pasture and making sure no animals used it. He'd mowed it himself last night, and the wedding rental company had set up every table, chair, and tent.

The wedding guests followed them, and as Charlotte looked out over the land that had brought them together, a deep sense of belonging strung through her, hooking her heart to Beau's. "This is just the beginning, isn't it, cowboy?"

Beau pulled her close, his voice full of promise. "Yes, little bird. The beginning of a beautiful, lifelong adventure."

She beamed at him as Sprout cried her excitement to see them. "I love you, Beau."

He kissed her properly this time, and Charlotte absolutely adored the touch of his lips against hers. "And I love you, Charlotte," he whispered.

Ahhh! Another Three Rivers Ranch romance novel! I'm so happy Beau got his happy ending with Charlotte, and I hope you are too. **Leave a review for them by scanning this QR code now!**

Read on for a sneak peek at the first novel in the Second Generation in Three Rivers Romance series — **THE COWBOY WHO CAME HOME** — and fall in love with Three Rivers as Finn Ackerman comes home after 11 years of military service!

Just turn the page!

Sneak Peek! The Cowboy Who Came Home Chapter 1

Edith Baxter nudged her horse forward while keeping her voice silent. She'd been working with Cocoa since the day Courage Reins had brought the beautiful bay to their stables. In fact, Peter Marshall, who owned this therapeutic riding facility, had called her and asked her to come help him train the horse for other clients.

She'd said yes immediately. She didn't get to work with as many horses as she'd like on her brother's farm, where she lived and wrote her children's books, where she took care of the house and all the smaller animals—and her brother.

He'd had a terrible time since the death of their cousin, and while Edith felt that loss too, she hadn't been as close to Carson as Alex had been.

She'd suffered a massive loss in her life too, and she'd been frequenting Courage Reins as a client since her return to Three Rivers three years ago.

Now, she shelved her thoughts, because being present

with a horse was a big part of riding. She couldn't forget for a single second that the beast upon whose back she sat could spook and spark at any moment. And Edith could end up with a broken back—or worse.

Cocoa had come a long way in the past couple of years, but she was still a horse. And horses had fickle personalities at the best of times, and this horse could *feel* what Edith felt.

So she couldn't think about Alex's troubles, or her own, while riding and guiding her. That was part of the therapy—the blessed release of thought. The fact that she didn't have to worry about the dirty dishes piling up in the sink, or the dozens of errands she needed to get done before businesses closed in town, or the fact that she lived mostly alone, on a ranch with her younger brother in a state she thought she'd never return to.

But for right now, she breathed in. She centered herself on Cocoa's back, right here on this tiny speck of land in a huge country, world, and universe.

Her fingers tingled, and she released her too-tight grip on the reins. Cocoa moved how she should've then, and Edith relaxed and smiled softly to herself. She could use this horse in a book now, and words and pictures flowed through her head as she moved Cocoa around the cone.

Getting the equines used to brightly colored objects was absolutely necessary, and Cocoa did great with the rest of the course. As Edith slid from the saddle so she could walk alongside Cocoa for her cooldown, the door to the observation room opened.

A cowboy stepped onto the dirt of the arena, his black

cowboy hat wide and smiling up on the edges. "You're both lookin' good," Peter Marshall said.

Edith trained her smile on him. "I know what you're going to say."

"Do you?" He grinned at her, because he was a tall, good-looking, happy-go-lucky, sensitive, perceptive man.

"You think Cocoa doesn't need me anymore."

"She doesn't."

"What if I need her?"

"You can choose any horse you want when you come for personal sessions."

Edith nodded and kept walking as Pete fell into step beside her. "You got a new horse?"

"Sure did."

"What's his name?'

"Reagan."

"He needs me?"

"He does."

Edith sighed, though it sure felt nice to be needed. Didn't everyone want to feel that way? Important? Special? Necessary? The last few years of Edith's life had put her in the top spot of "necessary" for so many people, and sometimes she craved a time where no one needed her. Or someone on whom *she* could rely on for everything, so *she* could have a weak hour, or day, or even a whole week.

"You don't see Margot when you come work with Cocoa," Pete said gently.

"Here we go," Edith said, cutting him a look out of the

corner of her eye. "I don't pay for these sessions. I'm not going to take Margot's time for free."

"Hm." That was Pete-speak for *You need it.*

And maybe she did. Edith wasn't opposed to counseling and therapy. With all she'd gone through in the past few years, talking to someone without any skin in her game had helped immensely. But so did training horses—and Pete paid her for that.

"I need this job," she said quietly. "And if you add on the counseling, then I feel like I have to pay, and then I'll ask you not to pay me." She looked over to him. "Alex's ranch does fine. It really does. But it's not like this place. We watch every dime."

Pete nodded like he understood. Maybe he did. Three Rivers Ranch spanned hundreds of acres and raised thousands of head of cattle. Pete's best friend, Squire Ackerman, owned and ran the ranch, but Pete had built and expanded his equine therapy unit here on the same property.

Bowman's Breeds, a rodeo horse training facility, also existed out on this ranch about forty-five minutes north of Three Rivers. They employed dozens of people, and everyone at Three Rivers went around and helped at other ranches during harvest, round-up, and branding. That was how Edith knew most of them; they'd come to help on her brother's ranch at crucial times of the year.

Edith had no idea what their financial situation was, but she'd been honest. Pete could do what he needed or wanted to do now.

"We have grant money to cover the full experience for

you," he said just as quietly as she'd spoken. "In fact, I *want* you to go through these sessions the same as a client would, so we can see how working with a specific horse and a specific counselor go together. Sometimes different counselors do better with different horses."

Edith thought about that for a beat. "I don't get that, but I believe you."

He chuckled, but he didn't go on to explain what he meant. Edith *had* been avoiding her counseling sessions when she came out to Courage Reins, so she couldn't argue with him there.

"All right," she drawled out. "I'll start seeing Margot."

"Well, actually." Pete darted his eyes to her now. "When you start working with Reagan, I'd like to pair him—and you—with...."

"Do not say Bull."

"Bull," Pete said almost on top of her last word. They looked at one another fully then, and with Cocoa plodding along beside them, they both laughed.

Edith let it cleanse her from the inside out, and as she quieted, a keen sense of peace and goodness filled her. She felt God watching over her and guiding her expertly in that moment, and she nodded.

"All right," she said in a firm, agreeable voice. "I'll work with Reagan and Bull."

"Your pay won't change."

"I can schedule extra sessions with Cocoa?" She reached over and ran her hand along the bay's side. "Would I have to see Margot if I do that?"

The cowboy sighed, which meant *yes*, but he said, "I'll leave that up to you."

She nodded, and the exit that led back to Cocoa's stable, where Edith would unsaddle her and brush her down and put her away for the day loomed only several paces ahead. Pete slowed to a stop. "Thank you, Edith. I sure appreciate you and all you do here."

"Thank you, Mister Marshall," she said diplomatically. "I love coming out here." She led Cocoa through the wide doorway and out of the arena. Fences stood guard on either side of the wide road, but they didn't obstruct her view of the homestead on this property.

She couldn't stop herself from glancing over to it and thinking about the boy she'd gone with in high school, albeit briefly.

Finley Ackerman. He'd been handsome and funny in high school, but their young love had been cut short when her family had moved to Florida. She'd seen him briefly over the summer after his first year of college too, but then he'd entered the Army, and Edith hadn't seen or spoken to him in almost a decade now.

She'd gone off to live her own life as a nanny back East. She'd started writing books there, after taking an internship with a publisher in New York City. All of that felt like a different life, that had happened to a different person.

Because there was Edith Before Levi and Edith After Levi.

She looked up into the sky, imagining she could see all the way to heaven. "I miss you so much sometimes," she whispered. "And other times, it's like we never met."

Edith didn't understand the human mind and heart as well as she'd like. She wished a clear blue sky, without a single cloud in sight, didn't make memories—good and bad—stream so readily through her mind.

She sometimes wished she didn't see whole stories in her head. That she wasn't so visual. That she didn't romanticize everything. But all of those things made her a very good author, and the publication of her children's books paid a lot of bills around the ranch.

She put Cocoa away properly, and in the shadows cast by the stable this afternoon, she leaned against the wood and checked her phone. She still had to fill out her paperwork for what she and Cocoa had done during their session, and she had a chapter to write in her current work-in-progress, but she just wanted a minute to catch up on the outside world.

She always put her phone in a locker when she trained, and all clients had to do the same. Cell phones and horses didn't go together at Courage Reins, something that allowed Edith the escape she craved when she came here. But she liked catching up too.

Alex had texted a couple of times, reminding her of the prescription she'd promised to pick up for him. She had a couple of emails that needed answering, one about the chicken feed she'd been trying to secure, and one about a library event in Amarillo.

She smiled as she read the invite to be one of the signing and speaking authors at this library's Summer Reading introduction event for patrons.

She'd love to do that, but she'd craft a professional acceptance email when she got home and got on her computer to handle her authoring business.

Everything else didn't matter, and Edith closed her phone and stowed it in her jeans pocket. She looked up and over to the row of cabins that lined an immaculately kept gravel path. Stables and barns lined this side, with the administration building for the ranch down to her right, and the homestead to her left. She didn't have any business with Three Rivers Ranch, but Courage Reins shared their stable facilities, so she came over here to get her horses.

A couple of cowboys came out of a cabin a couple down, and she lifted her hand in greeting as they saw her.

"Howdy, Edith," one said to her. "You comin' down to the homestead for dinner?"

She shook her head. "Nope, I've got a ton going on tonight." Plus, she had no idea why she'd ever go to the homestead here at Three Rivers Ranch for dinner. She hadn't been invited tonight either, and she didn't know what the occasion was. "But you guys enjoy."

Manny and Falcon continued on, and Edith figured she better finish up her work here and get going on the rest of her to-do list. So she returned to the big, glass-front Courage Reins building and filled out her paperwork.

"There you go," she said to Reese Sanders, who ran the office here at the facility.

"Thank you, Edith," he said without looking at the paper. "She do okay today?'

"She's amazing," Edith said, her voice brightening as she

spoke of Cocoa. She did love that horse, and she was going to miss her.

As she left the building, she took another moment to breathe in the mid-May air and look over to the homestead. It didn't look any different than she'd seen it before. A couple of unfamiliar trucks sat in the driveway, but so many people came out here to the ranch, and Edith certainly wouldn't know every vehicle that came here.

The grass shone green around the homestead, and she watched Beau Peterson, the current foreman at the ranch appear and climb the steps to the deep deck that spanned the width of the side of the house. He slid open the glass door and went right inside, and Edith wondered what that would be like. To have people coming and going from her private, personal residence all the time.

She'd asked Finn about it once, but he'd said he hadn't thought about it. That such a thing was just part of his life. He'd grown up with it, so it felt normal to him.

Edith reached up and removed the ponytail holder from her hair, and she ran her hands through it to get it to lay right. Now she felt ready to re-enter the normal world, the town and atmosphere away from Three Rivers Ranch, and she turned toward her SUV.

This place did have a vibe Edith had only ever felt here. Troubles and worries couldn't touch her here, but the moment she drove from dirt road to highway, the weight of her life would descend on her shoulders again.

"It's okay," she told herself as she started the car and

adjusted the air conditioning. "It's okay to have a real life and an escape. You can't live in la-la land forever."

A couple of hours helped her get through the week, and then she'd come back to Courage Reins and get away from everything all over again.

She pulled her phone from her pocket, where it didn't quite fit now that she'd sat down, and she put it in the middle console with her soda pop. That would be warm and flat by now, so Edith didn't reach for it. She liked her soda pop ice cold, fizzy, and flavored with grapefruit, lime, and orange.

Before she could twist to get her seatbelt on, someone knocked on the glass of her driver's side window. Edith spun that way as she both yelped and leaned away from the would-be attacker.

Her pulse sped through her bloodstream, and her adrenaline told her to find something she could use to ward off whoever had dared get so close to her, with only a simple pane of glass separating them.

But Edith kept her car neat, and all she had at her disposal was her phone. She forgot all about trying to grab it as she took in the terribly familiar features of the man on the other side of the glass.

Understanding and recognition kicked in, and Edith sat up straight and reached to roll down the window.

True, Finn now wore a beard, which he hadn't in high school or afterward. But his blue eyes sparkled with the smile on his face, and as the glass lowered, she heard his low chuckle.

That struck a familiar chord inside Edith too, and her own

smile formed. She pressed one hand to her still-flailing heartbeat. "Finn Ackerman. You scared me."

Sneak Peek! The Cowboy Who Came Home Chapter 2

Finley Ackerman couldn't believe who he was looking at. The gorgeous Edith Baxter. "I'm sorry," he said. "I didn't mean to. I just saw you, and I couldn't believe it, and...." He trailed off. "It's you." His back pinched because he had to lean down only slightly to see inside the SUV, and it wasn't a natural position. But he would not move. Oh, no, he would not.

Edith hadn't buckled in yet, and she opened the door. Finn got out of the way to allow her to stand, the moment between them tense and awkward. What did he do here? The last time he and Edith had been together, he'd kissed her. He hadn't known when he'd see her again, but he'd known he would.

The door closed, and Finn decided to do what was natural. He had no idea if she was married or seeing someone, but he moved into her personal space and took her into his arms. "Oh, wow. it's so good to see you."

She murmured, "It sure is," as she wrapped him up in her arms too. "What are you doing here?"

"I just got home," he said. "This morning. My momma is planning a big welcome home party tonight." He stepped back, ideas firing through his mind like machine gun shots. "You should come."

Edith's blue eyes widened, and she shook her head. "No, I don't think so."

"Why not?"

"I—" She looked over to the homestead, but Finn only had eyes for her. He couldn't look away, because he couldn't quite believe *Edith Baxter* stood in front of him. He'd seen her from the window that overlooked the ranch, and he'd left the cowboys his daddy had bribed into coming to help set up for the party mid-conversation. He'd have to answer for that, but for now, he simply basked in Edith's presence. Her beauty.

Her eyes came back to his. "I wasn't invited."

"I'm inviting you."

She shook her head again, that lovely blonde hair swaying with the motion. "I have a lot to do tonight." She scanned him down to his boots. "I can't believe you're here."

"I'm the one who lives here," he said. "I mean, sort of. For the next little while."

"Are you out of the Army then?"

"Yep." Finn rocked back onto his heels and shoved his hands in his jeans pockets. "I retired at my ten-year mark, and now...I'm here."

If that didn't scream, *I still don't know what my life should be*, Finn didn't know what would. He might as well have broadcast it from the speaker system and into the peace and serenity that still existed here at his family ranch.

"Well, welcome home." Edith smiled at him and tucked her hair behind her ear. "I'm glad you're here, safe and sound."

Finn was glad for that too, and he could talk for years and still not tell his friends and family everything he'd done in the past decade. Some of it he *couldn't* talk about.

"You seein' anyone?" He figured he might as well go straight for the bullseye. No sense beating around the bush, not when his attraction to this woman buzzed and fizzed through him. It popped and soared, and Finn needed to know if he could take her to dinner and when.

"No," she said.

"Married?"

"No." She shook her head again, those eyes shining like sapphires in a dark night. How could he have forgotten about her eyes?

"When can I take you out?" he asked.

Edith blinked at him, but Finn had learned in the Army to be direct. Maybe he was coming off a *little* strong. "I mean, I just got home, and I'll need to settle in, but I'd love to get your number, so when I'm sitting in front of my schedule, we can set something up."

Finn told himself to stop talking. He'd put a lot of words out there, and he just needed to *stop*. Edith looked like he'd hit her with a wet eel, and the cold water had just now started to spark with the electricity.

She blinked a couple of times, then opened her mouth only to promptly close it again. She once again looked back to the homestead, but Finn refused to do that. He could practically feel the eyes of this place on him. His momma's. Daddy's too, though he tended to leave Finn be until he had his lectures all planned out. The other cowboys. Heck, the building they stood in front of was filled with people who knew him and his parents, would be at the party tonight, and could see through each and every window—as the whole front was made of glass.

His skin itched to be somewhere no one could see him, but he couldn't walk away from Edith without getting her phone number. He wouldn't.

It had been a long time since Finn had been face-to-face with a woman who made his feet shift and his throat go dry. He cleared that as he tried to find solid ground beneath his boots, and he knew Edith saw and heard it all.

She gestured half-heartedly toward her car. "My phone's in there."

"You don't have your number memorized?" Finn teased, adding a smile to his face as he pulled his phone out so he could type her number into it. He focused on the screen for a moment, just long enough to put in his PIN and get the phone open. Then he looked at Edith again. "We can just...text. Talk. If you decide you don't want to go out with me, okay."

"It's been ten years," she said. "I just...don't even know where to start."

"How about with giving me your phone number?" He felt sparky and electric himself, and he hadn't had this much energy running through him in a long time. If ever. "Or I can give you mine, but you know, your phone is in there." He nodded toward her blue SUV.

"Good to see the Army didn't beat your humor out of you," she said dryly, placing one hand on her hip. That only accentuated her curves and caused Finn's smile to widen.

He tried to beat it back down. "Seriously," he said. "We don't have to go out. No pressure. But I'd love to catch up with you. Find out what these past ten years have been for you."

Something shuttered right over those eyes, and Finn wasn't sure what. He also didn't want to find out from his momma, though surely she knew. Ranch wives had a special network in Three Rivers, whether it was official or not, and his momma had been hovering around the gossip mill here in town for two and a half decades.

She'd know.

In fact, his phone chimed as a text from her popped up on his screen. Dread weighed down his chest on his next breath, because she'd asked, *Where did you go? We need you here to go over some things.*

He needed to get back before she sent out a search party. He looked up. "Where are you living? Maybe I'll just come by once all the hoopla of my coming home has died down."

Edith had folded her arms around herself, almost like she was trying to ward off a chill. *Or something bad*, he thought. Could that be him? Could she not feel this energy between them? How could that be one-sided?

It has been with other women, he reminded himself, and some of the bubbling attraction inside him grew cold too.

"I'm living with Alex," she said. "On a small ranch not far

from here, actually. It's called Coyote Pass. Not sure if you remember—"

"Oh, sure," Finn said as his Three Rivers memory fired at him. "Coyote Pass. We rode the horses down there one day, remember?" He burst out laughing, the sound of it going with this near-perfect almost-summer day. "Boy, was my daddy *mad*."

He was glad to be home, as everything felt so much lighter here. "Old Man Tompkins owned Coyote Pass. Wonder what happened to him."

"He passed," Edith said quietly, without all of the gusto and joviality Finn had laughed and spoken with. He wasn't sure why she seemed so melancholy about an old man passing away—especially one she surely couldn't have known or been close to. "His family went through everything, but no one wanted the ranch. They listed it for sale, and Alex...well, you know Alex. He has a gypsy soul, and he's wanted to return to Three Rivers since we left."

"I knew Alex once," Finn corrected gently. "Just like I knew you once." He exhaled as another text from his momma came in. He dared look toward the homestead, and sure enough, she stood on the deck now, one hand up to her forehead to shade her eyes as she scanned for him. Part of him wanted to duck down behind the cars here in the Courage Reins lot so she wouldn't see him. But the other part knew that wouldn't be enough. She'd find him, and fast.

"Ten years is a long time," he said, looking at Edith again. "I have to go. My momma wants me back at the homestead."

Edith looked that way too, and when her attention came back to his, she nodded. "Okay, here's my number." She rattled it off quickly, but Finn had fast, fast, fast fingers from his time behind keyboards. He recited it back to her; she nodded again; he tucked his phone away.

"It's so great to see you," he said again. "I mean, really, *really* great. You have no idea." Finn told himself not to get too carried away. He didn't need to confess all of his female failures in the first fifteen minutes of his reunion with Edith. He wasn't even sure it would become a reunion, his own attraction to her notwithstanding.

He couldn't just walk away either, so he lunged at her and took her into his arms again. "We'll talk soon, okay?" He swept his lips along her cheek and told himself to get out of there.

"Okay," ghosted behind him as he walked away, his eyes locked onto his mother's now. And oh, she'd have seen the beautiful blonde behind him and have multitudes of questions once Finn's boots ate up the distance between then.

Sure enough, he'd only just started up the steps to the deck when Momma asked, "Who was that?"

He'd be thirty-one years old in a couple of months, and he didn't have to hide an innocent kiss from his mother. He did wait until he'd reached the deck to say, "Edith Baxter, and I'm not talking about her."

His mother didn't frown the way she would've in high school. He was certainly old enough to date and fall in love now, and Edith had always been out of his league. That hadn't changed one whit, so Momma had no reason to be upset. Still, she looked back toward Courage Reins, which sat across the lawn and across the street to the west, something contemplative on her face.

"Are you going out with her?"

"Nope." Finn moved toward the door, because while it wasn't technically summer yet, the temperatures in Texas always hovered too high.

"Did you ask her out?" Momma asked.

"Yes." Finn opened the door and stepped into the blessed air conditioning. Several cowboys had been working, setting up tables and chairs, and most of them looked over to him. He wasn't sure what rode in their expressions, but he didn't like it. Pity, maybe? Reverence? Maybe simple wariness? He wasn't sure, and Finn just wanted to escape.

"She told you no?" Momma asked, her voice shocked.

"It was a short conversation, Momma," he said. "Because you kept texting me." He surveyed the tables and chairs. "You don't need me here."

"I do too," she said. "Daddy's going to be home with the bus any moment, and your brother will want to see you." She held her head high. "Plus, he picked up Grandma and Grandpa, and they're simply dying to hug you again." She gave him one of her piercing looks, and Finn really didn't want to disappoint his mother. "You just ran off mid-sentence, the boys said."

"Thanks, guys," Finn said dryly. That got the other cowboys to smile a little. "I just saw a pretty girl, and well, I knew her." He turned and looked out the window, but he didn't see Edith standing on the sidewalk, running her hands through her hair to get it to lay flat. He'd seen her do that so often in the past.

Yeah, high school, he told himself. And he was way past high school.

"At least I used to know her," he murmured to the trail of dust still hanging in the air, probably from Edith's car as she'd left the ranch. "Does she work at Courage Reins, Momma?"

"She does a little training for Uncle Pete, yes," Momma said, her voice wary.

"Who is it?" Beau asked as he came to stand next to Finn.

He looked at the foreman. "Edith Baxter."

"Oh, sure," Beau said easily. "She's real good with horses. Writes books about 'em and everything."

"Edith writes books?" Finn really had no idea who she was anymore, but a stinging, fizzing need to learn and re-learn everything about her started in his gut.

"Bus is here," Beau called next, and Finn blinked as the big yellow school bus filled his vision. His daddy drove it today, and the only reason Finn hadn't gone with him was because he hadn't wanted to put on a show. He didn't need all the kids fawning over him, or Sammy bursting into tears at the sight of him.

Of course, Momma had said Sammy had grown right up while Finn had been gone. He was almost eighteen now, and he'd graduate from high school in another couple of weeks. Oh, and he didn't go by *Sammy* anymore, but *Sam*.

As he stood there and watched the bus come to a stop and the kids who lived here at Three Rivers start to spill out of it, Finn wondered if there'd been another reason he hadn't gone with his daddy for the school bus pick-up. A reason he'd stayed here, that he'd *needed* to be here.

And that was to see and meet and talk to Edith again. Get her number. He slid his hand into his pocket and felt his device there, all while a feeling of goodness and rightness came over him.

It sure was good to be home.

And you won't make a fuss over your parents making a fuss over you.

The stern voice in his head reminded him of the General he'd worked under in Germany. There were no jokes while on duty in the intelligence department, and Finn had learned that quickly. The work they did there mattered, as it did in every department of the Armed Forces, but General Hutch did not allow for joviality. That could happen outside of the tactical room.

Finn watched the kids, ages five to eighteen, scatter toward the various houses and cabins out here on the ranch. Uncle Pete and Aunt Chelsea lived across the street, in the two-story house with the blue door, but Finn didn't see their youngest head that way.

Instead, Rich and Sam walked in through the garage door, both of them bellowing, "Where you at, Finny?" They laughed as Sam came through the doorway and into the kitchen first, and wow, Finn did not recognize him at all.

His hair had grown a little long, and it waved and curled in all directions. He had broad shoulders and stood as tall as Daddy now, with Momma's blue eyes shining at him as they crinkled with his smile.

"Sammy," he said, unable to censor himself. And then it didn't matter. It didn't matter that Sam was only his half-brother. That they only shared the same genes as their mother. That Finn had missed the last ten years of life here in Three Rivers, on this ranch, with his family.

He opened his arms and saw Sam's face fall, the crinkles for a whole new reason, a brand new emotion.

All Finn could feel was love. Love and acceptance and forgiveness. He'd relive Sam's life through the stories they'd tell each other over the next few days, weeks, months, and years.

"I missed you, brother," Finn whispered in Sam's ear as he held him tight, right against his chest. "I love you so much." His voice broke on the last word, and he couldn't even imagine the reunion he'd have with Mike and Libby.

They wouldn't be home in time for tonight's party, which meant Momma would simply have another one when they arrived. He wished he could've told her when he'd be arriving sooner, but the Army didn't exactly play by a Texas momma's timeline.

He'd found out yesterday that his flight would be that evening, and he'd land on the ranch this morning. And that was what had happened.

Libby had graduated from Faithview, a Christian college in Amarillo, and she now held a degree in ranch and business management. She hadn't come back to Three Rivers yet, because she wanted "outside experience." Those had been Momma's words, and Finn had only read them in an email. He could hear her voice as she said them, though, and Momma just wanted all of her chicks to come home.

Daddy had assured Finn multiple, multiple times that he'd always have a place at Three Rivers Ranch. Whenever he wanted it. In whatever capacity he wanted it. The problem was, Finn had no idea what he wanted.

Libby worked at another ranch as their general controller, and she claimed to really like Oklahoma. She couldn't just up and leave her job with only twelve hours' notice, and she'd said she'd talk to her boss about coming home for the weekend to see Finn.

Mike had just finished his junior year at Baylor, and he was off living the life Finn was pretty sure his momma had anticipated he'd live. He'd gone to Baylor for a year, but the environment simply hadn't suited him. He wondered if it would now, and he prayed that God would simply illuminate the path Finn should be on.

He hadn't yet, and Finn was starting to wonder if He ever would.

Then he thought of Edith standing on that sidewalk, in plain view, and Finn knew God loved him, cared about him, and had possibly shone a light on the first step Finn should take. Maybe.

Edith hadn't seemed all that keen to rush out to dinner with him that night. She'd even turned down his invitation for tonight's party.

In truth, Finn didn't want her to come to any of his welcome home shindigs, and relief filled him as he stepped back from Sam.

His younger brother wiped his eyes. "When's Mike coming home?"

"The weekend," Momma said, and Finn let her hug her youngest as he moved over to Rich.

"Look at you all grown up." He grinned at his cousin and hugged him too. "What's it like being the only kid at home?"

"It's not so bad," Rich said. "I mean, Daddy's not yelling at Henry all the time, so it's good." He grinned as he stepped out of Finn's arms. "You've got a beard."

Finn's hand went to it, and he grinned. "Yeah, I think it's nice."

"It looks great," Rich said.

"Your neck needs to be trimmed up," Momma said, her eyes appraising every little thing.

Finn simply grinned at her. "I'll do it for the family party this weekend. It'll just be a family thing, right?"

Momma didn't answer, which meant the weekend welcome home party could be as big as the one tonight. She'd invited everyone who lived or worked here on the ranch, and with the number of chairs they'd set up, Finn expected a big crowd.

"Finn, let's take a look at that closet door," Daddy said. He motioned to Finn from the mouth of the hallway, and Finn saw his escape.

"Sure thing." He headed that way, his eyes hooked on his father's. "Thanks," he murmured as he went past him into the darker, cooler, calmer hallway. He continued around the corner and down the steps to the basement, where he'd be living. Again.

He tried not to feel like he was moving backward. He wasn't. He'd taken control of his career in the Army, and he'd retired. He'd be thirty-one in a couple months, he had a decent amount of money saved, and the doors to his life were wide open.

If only he knew which one to walk through.

"Okay." Dad sighed as he walked into the basement bedroom where Finn had put his two duffle bags on the made and ready-to-sleep-in queen-sized bed. "Let's see if we can get this door to close all the way. It might just need a new knob."

Finn sat on the bed, then laid back between his bags. "What time is dinner tonight?"

"Your momma told everyone six."

"Six," Finn repeated.

"I told her not to expect more than an hour out of you."

"I can do it," Finn said, his voice quiet. His dad didn't respond, and only the sound of clicking came from the faulty doorknob. Finn closed his eyes, and he felt the serenity and peace that had always existed on this ranch, in this house.

"Dad, I'm really happy to be home." Finn's voice broke again, but he didn't care if his daddy heard it. He wanted them to know how glad he was to be there, how appreciative he was for their sacrifice, for having this bedroom ready for him at a moment's notice, for taking him in so completely.

Squire Ackerman had done that for Finn every day of his life since he'd met him when he was four years old. "I'm so glad you're my dad."

"I love you, son," Daddy said, and Finn's tears ran down

from the corners of his eyes toward his ears. "It's so good to have you home."

Finn took a big breath and steeled his nerves. "Now, it would be great if I could figure out what to do with my life."

Read **THE COWBOY WHO CAME HOME** right now — and fall in love with Three Rivers as Finn Ackerman and Edith Baxter are reunited after more than a decade apart! Just scan the code below and get this book!

Second Chance Ranch: A Three Rivers Ranch Romance™ (Book 1): After his deployment, injured and discharged Major Squire Ackerman returns to Three Rivers Ranch, wanting to forgive Kelly for ignoring him a decade ago. He'd like to provide the stable life she needs, but with old wounds opening and a ranch on the brink of financial collapse, it will take patience and faith to make their second chance possible.

Third Time's the Charm: A Three Rivers Ranch Romance™ (Book 2): First Lieutenant Peter Marshall has a truckload of debt and no way to provide for a family, but Chelsea helps him see past all the obstacles, all the scars. With so many unknowns, can Pete and Chelsea develop the love, acceptance, and faith needed to find their happily ever after?

Fourth and Long: A Three Rivers Ranch Romance™ (Book 3): Commander Brett Murphy goes to Three Rivers Ranch to find some rest and relaxation with his Army buddies. Having his ex-wife show up with a seven-year-old she claims is his son is anything but the R&R he craves. Kate needs to make amends, and Brett needs to find forgiveness, but are they too late to find their happily ever after?

Fifth Generation Cowboy: A Three Rivers Ranch Romance™ (Book 4): Tom Lovell has watched his friends find their true happiness on Three Rivers Ranch, but everywhere he looks, he only sees friends. Rose Reyes has been bringing her daughter out to the ranch for equine therapy for months, but it doesn't seem to be working. Her challenges with Mari are just as frustrating as ever. Could Tom be exactly what Rose needs? Can he remove his friendship blinders and find love with someone who's been right in front of him all this time?

Sixth Street Love Affair: A Three Rivers Ranch Romance™ (Book 5): After losing his wife a few years back, Garth Ahlstrom thinks he's ready for a second chance at love. But Juliette Thompson has a secret that could destroy their budding relationship. Can they find the strength, patience, and faith to make things work?

The Seventh Sergeant: A Three Rivers Ranch Romance™ (Book 6): Life has finally started to settle down for Sergeant Reese Sanders after his devastating injury overseas. Discharged from the Army and now with a good job at Courage Reins, he's finally found happiness—until a horrific fall puts him right back where he was years ago: Injured and depressed. Carly Watters, Reese's new veteran care coordinator, dislikes small towns almost as much as she loathes cowboys. But she finds herself faced with both when she gets assigned to Reese's case. Do they have the humility and faith to make their relationship more than professional?

Eight Second Ride: A Three Rivers Ranch Romance™ (Book 7): Ethan Greene loves his work at Three Rivers Ranch, but he can't seem to find the right woman to settle down with. When sassy yet vulnerable Brynn Bowman shows up at the ranch to recruit him back to the rodeo circuit, he takes a different approach with the barrel racing champion. His patience and newfound faith pay off when a friendship--and more--starts with Brynn. But she wants out of the rodeo circuit right when Ethan wants to rejoin. Can they find the path God wants them to take and still stay together?

The Ninth Inning: A Three Rivers Ranch Romance™ (Book 8): The Christmas season has never felt like such a burden to boutique owner Andrea Larsen. But with Mama gone and the holidays upon her, Andy finds herself wishing she hadn't been so quick to judge her former boyfriend, cowboy Lawrence Collins. Well, Lawrence hasn't forgotten about Andy either, and he devises a plan to get her out to the ranch so they can reconnect. Do they have the faith and humility to patch things up and start a new relationship?

Ten Days in Town: A Three Rivers Ranch Romance™ (Book 9): Sandy Keller is tired of the dating scene in Three Rivers. Though she owns the pancake house, she's looking for a fresh start, which means an escape from the town where she grew up. When her older brother's best friend, Tad Jorgensen, comes to town for the holidays, it is a balm to his weary soul. A helicopter tour guide who experienced a near-death experience, he's looking to start over too-- but in Three Rivers. Can Sandy and Tad navigate their troubles to find the path God wants them to take--and discover true love--in only ten days?

Eleven Year Reunion: A Three Rivers Ranch Romance™ (Book 10): Pastry chef extraordinaire, Grace Lewis has moved to Three Rivers to help Heidi Ackerman open a bakery in Three Rivers. Grace relishes the idea of starting over in a town where no one knows about her failed cupcakery. She doesn't expect to run into her old high school boyfriend, Jonathan Carver. A carpenter working at Three Rivers Ranch, Jon's in town against his will. But with Grace now on the scene, Jon's thinking life in Three Rivers is suddenly looking up. But with her focus on baking and his disdain for small towns, can they make their eleven year reunion stick?

The Twelfth Town: A Three Rivers Ranch Romance™ (Book 11): Newscaster Taryn Tucker has had enough of life on-screen. She's bounced from town to town before arriving in Three Rivers, completely alone and completely anonymous--just the way she now likes it. She takes a job cleaning at Three Rivers Ranch, hoping for a chance to figure out who she is and where God wants her. When she meets happy-go-lucky cowhand Kenny Stockton, she doesn't expect sparks to fly. Kenny's always been "the best friend" for his female friends, but the pull between him and Taryn can't be denied. Will they have the courage and faith necessary to make their opposite worlds mesh?

Lucky Number Thirteen: A Three Rivers Ranch Romance™ (Book 12): Tanner Wolf, a rodeo champion ten times over, is excited to be riding in Three Rivers for the first time since he left his philandering ways and found religion. Seeing his old friends Ethan and Brynn is therapuetic--until a terrible accident lands him in the hospital. With his rodeo career over, Tanner thinks maybe he'll stay in town--and it's not just because his nurse, Summer Hamblin, is the prettiest woman he's ever met. But Summer's the queen of first dates, and as she looks for a way to make a relationship with the transient rodeo star work Summer's not sure she has the fortitude to go on a second date. Can they find love among the tragedy?

The Curse of February Fourteenth: A Three Rivers Ranch Romance™ (Book 13): Cal Hodgkins, cowboy veterinarian at Bowman's Breeds, isn't planning to meet anyone at the masked dance in small-town Three Rivers. He just wants to get his bachelor friends off his back and sit on the sidelines to drink his punch. But when he sees a woman dressed in gorgeous butterfly wings and cowgirl boots with blue stitching, he's smitten. Too bad she runs away from the dance before he can get her name, leaving only her boot behind...

Fifteen Minutes of Fame: A Three Rivers Ranch Romance™ (Book 14): Navy Richards is thirty-five years of tired—tired of dating the same men, working a demanding job, and getting her heart broken over and over again. Her aunt has always spoken highly of the matchmaker in Three Rivers, Texas, so she takes a six-month sabbatical from her high-stress job as a pediatric nurse, hops on a bus, and meets with the matchmaker. Then she meets Gavin Redd. He's handsome, he's hardworking, and he's a cowboy. But is he an Aquarius too? Navy's not making a move until she knows for sure...

Sixteen Steps to Fall in Love: A Three Rivers Ranch Romance™ (Book 15): A chance encounter at a dog park sheds new light on the tall, talented Boone that Nicole can't ignore. As they get to know each other better and start to dig into each other's past, Nicole is the one who wants to run. This time from her growing admiration and attachment to Boone. From her aging parents. From herself.

But Boone feels the attraction between them too, and he decides he's tired of running and ready to make Three Rivers his permanent home. **Can Boone and Nicole use their faith to overcome their differences and find a happily-ever-after together?**

The Sleigh on Seventeenth Street: A Three Rivers Ranch Romance™ (Book 16): A cowboy with skills as an electrician tries a relationship with a down-on-her luck plumber. Can Dylan and Camila make water and electricity play nicely together this Christmas season? Or will they get shocked as they try to make their relation-

ship work?

The First Lady of Three Rivers Ranch: A Three Rivers Ranch Romance™ (Book 17): Heidi Duffin has been dreaming about opening her own bakery since she was thirteen years old. She scrimped and saved for years to afford baking and pastry school in San Francisco. And now she only has one year left before she's a certified pastry chef. Frank Ackerman's father has recently retired, and he's taken over the largest cattle ranch in the Texas Panhandle. A horseman through and through, he's also nearing thirty-one and looking for someone to bring love and joy to a homestead that's been dominated by men for a decade. But when he convinces Heidi to come clean the cowboy cabins, she changes all that. But the siren's call of a bakery is still loud in Heidi's ears, even if she's also seeing a future with Frank. Can she rely on her faith in ways she's never had to before or will their relationship end when summer does?

Second Generation in Three Rivers Romance™ Series

Step back into the heartwarming small Texas town of Three Rivers! This beloved town has captured the hearts of 2.5 million readers and caught the eye of Sony Pictures, and now a new generation of cowboys and cowgirls is ready to take center stage. Scan the QR code below with your phone to check out this new series!

1. The Cowboy Who Came Home - featuring Squire's son, Finn from SECOND CHANCE RANCH!

2. The Cowboy Who Looked Again - featuring Bear Glover's son, Lincoln, from THE MECHANICS OF MISTLETOE!

Seven Sons Ranch in Three Rivers Romance™ Series

Meet the cowboy billionaire brothers at Seven Sons Ranch! Scan the QR code below with your phone to check out this complete series.

1. Rhett
2. Tripp
3. Liam
4. Jeremiah
5. Wyatt
6. Skyler
7. Micah
8. Gideon

Shiloh Ridge Ranch in Three Rivers Romance™ Series

Meet the cowboy billionaires in the southern hills outside of Three Rivers! Scan the QR code below with your phone to check out this complete series.

1. The Mechanics of Mistletoe
2. The Horsepower of the Holiday
3. The Construction of Cheer
4. The Secret of Santa
5. The Gift of Gingerbread
6. The Harmony of Holly
7. The Chemistry of Christmas
8. The Delivery of Decor
9. The Blessing of Babies
10. The Networking of the Nativity
11. The Wrangling of the Wreath
12. The Hope of Her Heart

About Liz

Liz Isaacson writes inspirational romance, usually set in Texas, or Wyoming, or anywhere else horses and cowboys exist. She lives in Utah, where she writes full-time, takes her two dogs to the park everyday, and eats a lot of veggies while writing. Find her on her website at feelgoodfictionbooks.com